Gravity

Michael Davis

Gravity

stories

Carnegie Mellon University Press • Pittsburgh 2009

Acknowledgments

Grateful acknowledgment is made to editors in whose magazines these stories first appeared:

The Black Mountain Review, Chicago Quarterly Review, Eclipse, The Georgia Review, Hayden's Ferry Review, The Mid-American Review, Storyglossia, and *Willow Springs*

The author is also extremely grateful for help provided by the following people in making this collection a reality: Gerald Costanzo, Richard Katrovas, Jaimy Gordon, Robert Eversz, Stuart Dybek, and Emilie Parry.

Book design: Connie Amoroso

Library of Congress Control Number 2008940120
ISBN 978-0-88748-508-4

10 9 8 7 6 5 4 3 2 1

Contents

for my parents
Glover and Sandra Davis

Living in It

Tomlin sits across from me. Pissed. He wants to smoke a cigarette, but he doesn't do that anymore, and anyway we're in the café of the Cherry Blossom Hotel. Tomlin's got a tonsure of white around the back of his head but nothing on top. That's the first thing you notice. Then the liver spots. Gigantic ones that might as well be birthmarks or bruises for all anybody knows or cares. He's of an indeterminate ancientness. He'd gouge holes in the ground if he thought the earth could feel the pain. It's freeing, really. It almost makes me happy. Fifteen minutes with him and I feel fortified, ready to go back and face one more day of blocked-up toilets and garbage. I sip my lousy coffee and smoke down to the filter. I crush the butt out on my shoe, and nobody needs to understand.

The Kitchen Staff watches us from behind the coffee counter. Three women who used to work the x-ray machine at the airport. They are harder than pig iron and they stick together. They'll beat you. I've seen them facedown snarling dogs with just a chair, a broken bottle, and some language. Glaring over the espresso machine, they look offended by our existence, enraged, as if they can read our thoughts, sure that we come here just to stink up the place and make their lives harder. They comprehend all, see all. And what they see, they despise.

We are your filth-ridden, smoking co-workers.

We are having a cup of coffee. We excremental examples

anyway."

"Well, maybe I'll feed it."

"The fuck you will. You'll forget or your wife'll start having nightmares and chop it up while you're at work."

"Maybe I'll get two, then. And hide one. So when she kills the first one, I can tell her Jesus raised it from the dead."

Tomlin sighs, stares into his coffee cup.

We are emotional janitors.

I look to Tomlin as my moral compass. He's an atheist, he says, which means he can't pray; he can only hope—for a global nuclear war. He'll smile and wink and say it's best for everybody. Square the books. Take it back to before humans got out of control and became an infestation. He's one of the few people who'll be happy when all that's left is smoking ash and twisted rebar. It's an interesting approach to the world. How bad can things seem if you're ready to burn at any given moment? Still, Tomlin says it's not going to matter when some crazy fool rolls a hundred pounds of diesel into the Blossom's lobby and lets the bitch burn. He says the world is becoming a disease-ridden corpse. Eventually, we're all going to have to face the consequences. Tomlin is also fond of reminding me that, in lieu of a redeeming bullet in the back of the head, a good low-carbon straight razor costs $5.78. Applying it to one's own throat costs nothing.

The Kitchen Staff snaps the TV off with their remote.

"One of these days," Tomlin says, "I'm going to take an axe handle to that espresso machine."

I nod slowly and glare at the Kitchen Staff with a fierceness.

"What about this," he says. "Get a horned viper. A horned viper can bite you and you'll just go to sleep. No pain. Dead in seconds."

"That's a myth."

Tomlin looks at me and raises his eyebrows.

Of all the venomous snakes in Africa, Tomlin, Otis, and I have learned that the horned viper is actually the least likely to bite a human. We know this because the high school football team that stayed up on the twelfth floor five months ago left one in a bathtub. Marciel has a phobia about snakes, and so naturally he's the one who found it when he went up to unclog the toilet. Since then, the rest of us have done a few snake searches on the internet, and Marciel has stayed as drunk as possible. He's still going to the Evangelical Spiritual therapist, who told him the snake was a physical manifestation of the Devil—but added that it's natural to feel anxiety about Satan and that we shouldn't sublimate our emotions. I don't think Evangelical therapy has been helping Marciel much considering all the sublimating he's been doing with the apricot brandy he takes from the kitchen.

My cell phone rings. It's Beth, so I ignore it. It has been something of a general policy of mine not to answer when it's Beth. She hired a private investigator a year ago to find out all about our boy. He lives in Arizona now. He's in preschool. His name is Robert. I discover her in bed some days, holding the phone to her chest, dial tone carrying out of the receiver, and I wonder was she calling his house again. Our son. Not our son. I've stopped asking. Maybe I wonder sometimes how it might feel not to have to come home to this.

In two minutes—less than 113 seconds to be exact—I will have to go get Otis and check out the drainpipes on the mountainside where the hotel plumbing is supposed to empty out. Otis tells me we're expected to wear hip boots for the job, which does not bode well.

Garth beeps Tomlin on his walkie-talkie and they have a conversation about the roach problem in the second floor east wing. Guests are upset. Garth is pissed, screaming, his angry little voice coming through the two-way like some kind of Lilliputian tent preacher. But years in the janitorial profession have taught Tomlin to breathe and be the Zen master who speaks calmly and in short syllables. He is Master Po. Master Tomlin, the Silently Angry.

"No," he says. "Yes. I understand. Right."

"Can't you just tell him they're authentic roaches from Shanghai?"

Tomlin says nothing. He gets up and stalks away, a grim expression on his face.

I pick up our half-full Styrofoam cups and walk through the café. It's made to look like an ornamental Chinese garden complete with fake bamboo, red paper lamps, black lacquered tables, and an artificial stream that works 50 percent of the time. Koi can't live in it, we've discovered. On my way out, I place the cups right on the inside of the café's round wooden door. Ten-to-one, when some guest walks through it, rancid coffee will go everywhere. Two-to-one, Tomlin will be culling the roaches and Marciel will be sleeping off a pint of sublimation. That means I will get the call, because the Kitchen Staff has made it abundantly clear they can't be bothered with spills. It means I'll have to take the hip boots off and hightail it back up the mountain. Sorry, Otis. You should have prayed more to the Muse.

Abundantly clear. Some things just are. Like the fact that the local villagers of Pine Bluff, Colorado, have no idea what to make of the Blossom. Actually, let's be real. Nobody has any idea what to make of it—not even Garth, if you decide to qualify him as a person.

Architecturally, it's about as bogus as a hotel can get, a series of interconnected towers made from cheap concrete and gridded into floors. When I was fifteen, my uncle took me to a donkey bar in Tijuana that looked like that: a parking structure closed off and painted in bright primary colors. The Blossom is essentially the same thing without the donkey. Instead, for lovers of wildlife, there's the crazed grizzly bear who Tomlin named Claudia, after his first wife, and who occasionally puts the fear of god into the guests by trashing their vehicles in front of them.

In aesthetic terms, the main differences between the Blossom and a donkey bar come down to a few green, tiled dragon corners and fake round windows that help create a sort-of pagoda *façade*. Ergo, Chinese hotel. Ergo, occasional Pine Bluffians coming halfway up the mountain road or watching from the tree line, bewildered expressions on their faces. Standing in my hip boots, covered in human and animal fecal matter, I have stared back, painfully aware that the tree line was not the only divider between my world and theirs— and burdened with the knowledge that the Blossom presides over everything like the last remaining ruin of an abandoned theme park, a dead world devoted to particleboard and leakage, cheap moldings and graft.

But let's go with the idea of abundance, get right to the heart of it: me and Otis working our way down the side of the mountain with climbing ropes to unplug the sewer so the waste can run down the mountainside, through the forest, and into town like it's supposed to. The sewage pipe is about two hundred feet below, sticking straight out of the earth like a busted rib. And here's Garth on the walkie-talkie: "Where are you, Otis? Otis? Give me your *exact* coordinates." Garth is worried. Garth has had more than his usual four Red Bulls this afternoon. Maybe a fun line of cocaine up his nose. Maybe two.

He walks around most days in a brown silk robe, Ming Dynasty style with matching slippers, high, trying to look like Wise Old Grandfather. Needless to say, Garth is 36, a straight-up white boy from Hackensack. The closest he's probably come to China has been the Nee-Hou Restaurant in Trenton. But on a mountain in Colorado, maybe that's enough. In the nineteen months of The Blossom's history, the only affectation Garth has missed is the long Emperor Ming fingernails, which he's probably growing right now while Otis and I risk our lives for plumbing.

"We can see it," Otis says into the two-way. "We have visual confirmation." He slides a little lower on the line and hammers a piton between two boulders.

"Why do you talk like that?"

Otis cranes his neck so he can glare up at me. "Don't trip, Ellis."

"I heard what you said. You said, 'visual confirmation.'"

"You're trippin', Ellis. Don't trip."

"Oh, I get it. Now you're all *trippin boo*, but a minute ago you were, 'Check. Roger. Visual target in sight, captain.'"

"Fuck you."

I laugh my hard laugh. I almost find him funny. I wonder if Otis is going to find it funny when I get to climb back up the line and he has to pipesnake the drain all by his lonesome. I'll sure as shit be laughing then.

We secure ourselves on either side of the drain. This is accomplished by running nylon ropes through carabiners in Velcro waist harnesses that look like diapers. We're wearing hip boots because, once we clear the drain, the nastiness will spray out like Hell's own Trevi Fountain. For chest coverage, we're wearing brown plastic trash bags. This is because, according to Tomlin (who's done it before all by himself), it's impossible to get the sewage completely out of rain slickers, coveralls, or hair. Otis pulls down his goggles and begins to unfold the deluxe fourteen-foot pipe snake.

I look down and imagine jumping. On his list of the twenty best ways for maintenance workers to die, Tomlin has defined number eleven as drowning in a water tower cistern filled with Bushmills single malt. Such a way to die would be, in the words of our beloved employer, the "quintessence of decadence." With Garth, everything's the quintessence of, indubitably, without a doubt, the paragon of, essentially.

In the world according to Garth, there are stylish ways to die and gauche ones, some flamboyant, others plain. Strange words from the man who pretends to be a different ethnicity to up his booking rate. But Garth doesn't know what Tomlin claims to know: there may only be good ways to die, although some may be better than others. Right now, dangling from a rope for the sake of someone else's shit, I can't think of a better exit than a lungful of County Antrim's finest.

I'm waiting on the café spill call to save me, but it never comes. This means Otis sits on my right shoulder like a baby at the zoo—a large, bald two hundred fifty pound baby, smelling of old cigarillos, in hip boots and a trash bag. I've got my own goggles on now because I'm the anchorman. And I really hope this works out since I'm staring right into the mouth of the pipe.

The pipe snake looks like a giant segmented bottle cleaner with a corkscrew at the tip. Otis works it in, giving it an angry twist every few inches.

"I hate this job," he says.

"This job hates *you*."

"You been hanging around Tomlin too much. Pretty soon, we'll be out here looking for your body."

"Don't talk trash, Otis. Tomlin knows things. He *knows* things. You should listen to the man speak."

"I listened to him," says Otis, twisting the pipe snake almost all the way in. "Aha. Found the motherfucker."

"You listened to him. But you didn't *hear him.*"

I bend my knees and get ready to push off to the side. Otis will push off of me. And, if all goes well, the blocked-up shit will fire out between us. If all doesn't go well, my plan is to at least keep my mouth closed.

"Tomlin never said much to me other than I should blow myself up for science," he says.

We re-thread the ropes and get ready. I coil up as much energy as I can in my legs. Otis puts his left boot against my right shoulder, holds his line with one hand and yanks the pipe snake out with the other. We leap apart. A few hundred pounds of raw sludge goes into the air between us with a hiss. Aside from being coated by a fine sewer mist, Otis and I are mostly unviolated. We wait for the pressure to die down to a garden hose dribble before starting the slow climb back.

"You really think Tomlin knows a lot about science and cadavers and that?"

A few moments pass before Otis finds the energy to say, "Ellis, that's just stupid."

Beth has her friend, Lenorah, over with Lenorah's two kids, Nell and Illy. I don't know what the kids' actual names are. Probably Nelson and Illyana. But who's asking? The important thing is that, if the local toddler contingent is going to be represented, the local septuagenarian population should be present as well—namely Tomlin. He sits with a cup of coffee in the corner of the living room at our computer desk, surfs the net, and talks about as often as I do, which is to say, little. As Beth's husband, I am required to sit right up next to the kids on the couch. I'm required to participate in socialization with my wife's new friends, all of whom are fundamentalist Christians in their thirties with children under the age of ten. And they always get around, sooner or later, to the fact that we gave up our boy for adoption.

Tonight, it's Lenorah: the sighing, coo-cooing, Jesus-loving center of the universe and her perpetually screaming, defecating offspring. But so be it. I got home from my mountaineering adventure, wanting nothing more than to shower off the corruption and go to sleep, only to find Lenorah T-minus fifteen minutes and counting. Enough time to entertain running to the car and flooring it or perhaps a few choice suicide fantasies. Enough time to say, "So be it," over and over before calling Tomlin. I can always depend on the old smilodon to be free and available, even though to save face he has to say something like, "Well, I don't know. I might have something going on. You'll have to call me back." Just like a schoolgirl. I usually call him later, and whatever it was has mysteriously fallen through.

Lenorah wrinkles up her nose and pokes Illy in the stomach. "Say Jesus loves me," Lenorah says. "Say Jesus." Illy gurgles "Jeegis," before letting go in her diaper and trying to fit her fist in her mouth. Beth and Lenorah rejoice and laugh hysterically. Praise Jesus for such a cute kid. But Illy and I look at each other, and we know: just get the job done. That's all life can ask. Say Jesus. Then it's all right. Then you can load your diaper with a modicum of grace.

Much wooden laughter and baby talk from Beth and Lenorah. Though occasionally they shoot each other highly critical, calculating looks. I wonder if my wife and her friend actually get along or if there's some unspoken agreement that all fundamentalists must act like distant relatives meeting each other for the first time. Tomlin lets out a belch or my attention wavers, and I see Beth take on a different, yet equally critical, expression—the severe, smoking look of death that a wife usually reserves for younger, firmer women who may be trying to adhere to her man. However, when filth is adhering to your man ten hours a day, it appears that you get to save those looks for him and his buddies.

So be it.

Actually, I am rather undead. With every conversation about the goodness of adoption, I see Beth get a little more fundamentalist. As in "sinking into the fundament." Buried in it. Brain-deep. She gets fundy and I get zombie. Now the process is almost complete for both of us. I sit, a faint smile on my face, and appreciate the kids. In instances where there are no kids, I nod seriously at Beth's friends and make the little noises people make when they're listening. I am allowed one beer. If I put on an especially convincing show, Beth will be satisfied that I've done my part and go to bed early, avoiding accusations, weeping, and the invocation of our Lord and Redeemer to brutally show me the error of my ways.

But I know the error of my ways.

"Here you go, Ellis," says Tomlin. "Here's your fuckin' snake."

There's a general gasp from the couch. Tomlin points to the picture of a bright green snake with ruby eyes on the computer screen. He has no idea that all the stained glass windows in all the churches of the world just shattered at once. Lenorah hisses the way I imagine the snake would if someone called up a picture of a human in its living room and uttered something profane. She yanks Illy into the bathroom to change her diaper, and Illy starts crying.

I don't want to look at Beth, so I look at Nell. He grins, and I count six teeth in his mouth, three spaced on the bottom and three together on the top. He's looking at the snake.

"See that shit?" Tomlin winks at the boy and slurps some coffee. "That's a fuckin' emerald tree boa. You like that?"

Nell nods his empty little head and keeps grinning.

"I think you're leaving now," Beth says to Tomlin, and I know she's gone pale the way she does right before she starts to shake from too much stress.

Lenorah comes back and says, "No, I think *we're* leaving." She takes Nell by the hand and carries Illy out the door. Over Lenorah's shoulder, Illy waves at me with the fist that was too large for her mouth. I wave back. In her own way, Illy's telling me, *let's face it, tonight there will be crying.* And in my way, I'm saying *yes, I know.* She looks at me with big, mournful blue eyes and a tiny part of me, deep down, a tiny non-zombified centimeter, feels moved—one worker to another, Illy and I, we understand each other.

"What do you think you're doing?" Beth expects me to do something about the fact that Tomlin just belched, called up another emerald tree boa on the screen, and cackled like the snake was some kind of dirty joke and he finally got the punch line.

"I'm waving at the kid."

We look at each other for a moment before Beth stalks into the bedroom and shuts the door. There will be reprisals. There will be screaming. I wait and say "So be it" to the carpet twenty or thirty times, sensing my zombification reassert itself, willing it to rise up and take away that last bit of me that might want to start screaming, too. I feel as if I'm slowly turning to stone or, given my life, at least a low-grade cement statue of a janitor. And I say, so be it. That's all right. I've done my part, my screaming.

This was before Beth had her breakdown. I screamed a lot before she had it, the complete and utter psychotic rip down the center of her brain. The way I imagine it—like the window of an airplane getting punctured at altitude—the contents of her mind sucked out the hole with so much hiss. And then she woke up one day. But she didn't wake up. And she realized I was there, had been waiting there. But she didn't realize. And she found Jesus. And she refurnished the interior of her brain. But I'm not fond of the décor.

I say: so be it, and everything's okay. The adventures of statues are many and various. Statues get to be left alone in this world and probably have fewer problems. There's always a place for statuary. And the successful ones get put in the Louvre. So there really is no glass ceiling when it comes to a statue's upward mobility. Glass walls, maybe.

"That didn't take long," grins Tomlin. He whacks his paper coffee cup down beside the computer keyboard, and I realize his teeth are not that different from Nell's. "Now we can get down to business. Did you know you can buy these bitches with a credit card right now?"

In the end, I bought four. Four snakes and no more room on the MasterCard. That's it. I winced before I hit CONFIRM TRANSACTION but, according to Tomlin, if you're going to ruin your credit, you might as well do it on emerald tree boas from the Amazon basin. And, goddamn it, he's right. Thank Jesus. Or don't. I've been walking around all day with one of them in the sleeve of my pink-orange coveralls. It's wrapped around my arm, and it likes it there. I address it as Satan. I refer to the others as Maltodextrin, Cleano, and Colorado State Birding Trail as these were words I randomly noticed in the break room when I came to work. But Satan is my favorite.

For his part, Marciel talks Spanish to the Devil while pushing a housekeeper's cleaning cart down the halls, telling the Prince of Darkness to get away, get back, get behind him. And Marciel gives me nervous looks whenever I go by. Maybe he's seen snaky lumps shift and tighten under my coverall sleeves. Maybe he's looked into my face and seen an emerald swamplight there with zombies and snakes—thoughts of my marriage like a half-sunk raft stuck with mosquitoes. The Blossom is there, too, in my eyes, in the center of my swamp, its dragon corners enfolded in a dirty gauze of webs and vines, creepers and mold.

The night of Lenorah's visit, I sleep little and drink much.

The next day, Beth moves in with her parents in Boulder for a week of complaining and prayer.

Then the snakes move in and Beth moves back.

For the love of sweet whiskey I've slept with my new reptilian friends in the Caprice since her return. Seven holy days of snakes and Bushmills, of plungers and mops in the blear-eyed stuporous day, and feeding live white mice to the boas at night. Stretched out on the Caprice's backseat, staring up at parking lot lights, I want to jump on Jesus, beat him senseless, and raise my angry little fists to heaven. I want to dive into a cistern of Bushmills and find the mystical portal to County Antrim. To join the Devil's army and execute the helpless. To load my diaper and hold my breath. The whiskey itself is a serpent, a burning firesnake twisting into my lungs and coiling around my heart.

The snakes move on the seats of the Caprice, slither over the headrests. The mice don't stand a chance. I've been able to tell Satan apart by the blue-gray stripe across his nose. But when he strikes, he's invisible, like the others. All week, I sat in the backseat while my new friends slid over my thighs. It's been a weird experience—being part of the hunting landscape.

This is what Pine Bluff feels when Garth goes out in his war chariot with his bow like the Emperor Ming of old.

Today, Garth has called the maintenance staff to accounts, to an inquest of sorts. We stand before his mahogany desk—Marciel, Otis, Tomlin, and me, all covered in different degrees of filth. Garth presses his fingertips together. His long nails are coming in nicely. His blond Fu Manchu has gotten downright respectable. He's wearing a brown satin cap with Chinese characters on it and a yellow T-shirt that says *Boston Marathon 1988*.

"You people," says Garth, "have no values. No value system. No guiding functions. You're acting like peasants."

In the normal course of human events, when someone addresses a group with "You people," a certain amount of hostility results. The phrase conjures up white-columned houses and tobacco plantations, red-faced state governors and chain gangs. Nobody wants to be "You people." But my fellow sanitation engineers just sigh at their shoes, perhaps even in agreement. Peasants. Even Tomlin, especially Tomlin. What I took as Zen remove, as the calm Master Po-ness of one who's seen it all and is now wise beyond his station, is proving to be nothing more than tiredness, resignation, peasantry. It feels like a general, unspoken agreement that, yes, we all suck—not just because we're janitors, but because we're low-down human specimens.

Maybe we *should* blow ourselves up for science.

"You need iron balls to be in hotels. IRON. You know what iron is, Ellis?"

I nod. I also know what unemployment is and hate myself for knowing it while nodding.

"Now we have a fucking roach problem, second floor east. And five guests have left. Whose fault is that? Mine? You guys fucked up. The roaches haven't fucked up. The roaches are doing their jobs. They're on-task. That means you guys are, right now, lower than the fucking roaches."

Garth's eyes are bugging out slightly from whatever stimulant has frothed him up to this angry place. His blond Fu Manchu vibrates as he talks. That Garth is a strange cat is beyond question. Maybe, at one point, the whole ancient

Chinese motif was a put-on. But somewhere along the path toward having us pull his war chariot through the forest so he could shoot arrows at deer, Garth crossed over. He swivels around and sprinkles some incense on the hot iron brazier behind his desk. Then he presses his fingers back together and looks over them.

"You need direction." He nods to himself. "You need a guiding philosophy."

Just like the war chariot, his office is done up in red and gold. The black wrought iron incense brazier hangs down to desk level by a chain. A jade luck dragon slithers across the front edge of his desk. And a *Webster's New Collegiate Dictionary* always sits in an ornate wooden bookstand from the Eastern Han Dynasty, open to the word of the day.

We know about these artifacts because Garth takes the time to explain them. He'll call one of us in to talk about, say, a forgotten puddle of vomit or a mess left by Claudia, Tomlin's favorite grizzly bear, who likes to rip off trunk hoods and upend cars. Garth will begin in a coked-out furor—all twisted up about how the puke bonded with the hallway carpet at the molecular level and how now everything needs to be ripped out or how Claudia couldn't get to a bag of dog food and wound up flipping a Corolla down the mountainside in frustration. But Garth's lectures invariably end with: *This is an authentic. AUTHENTIC. Vhazz from the time of Cao Cao. Look at it. See that crack? That was made when Hua Tuo delivered his famous speech on the significance of the sunrise.* Like that. Garth knows what he's talking about, as far as any of us can tell. We stopped trying to cross-check him with the internet long ago.

So, when he hands each of us a new copy of Sun Tzu's *The Art of War*, we hold it in our hands and blink and nod. We're lower than the fucking roaches, but we can read *The Art of War*.

"Simply put," he says, "this is battle. This is conflagration. Chaos. Life is a struggle and you people—maybe not you, Tomlin—but the rest of you fuckers have no idea what's going on. You're stupid. You're lazy. And you're your own and the Blossom's worst enemies." Garth sniffs. His pupils are tiny.

I'd like to say I've never been spoken to like this, that

I've got a smudge of self-respect left on my zombie heart, but I look at my shoes like everyone else. This isn't the first of Garth's speeches we've had to enjoy. I'm thinking about Satan, who's traveled up my right arm and coiled around my shoulder. Marciel, looking as contrite as an altar boy, is doubtless dreaming about apricot sublimation or the Prince of Darkness, while Tomlin imagines everyone dead and Otis tries not to trip. But we all look sufficiently browbeaten by the time Garth takes another breath.

"One thing I want for you. One thing—no matter if you keep this job or not—is for you to pull yourselves up. Take responsibility for once in your sorry lives." He sits back and wipes sweat from under his eyes even though the room is cool and smells of purple lotus. "So I need two things. One, no cockroaches on second floor east. Two, this immortal manual for life and warfare read by this day next week. There will be a test, and then we'll see who keeps his job. Now fuck off." Garth puts his feet up on his desk and closes his eyes, exhausted.

Tomlin takes a cigarette out of the pack on the desk and puts it between Garth's parted lips. Otis lights it. Without opening his eyes, Garth blows a funnel of smoke over his head, where it mingles with the incense. We file silently out of the room and Marciel shuts the door softly behind us. I turn the book over, and read the back: *An immortal manual for life and warfare written by perhaps the greatest military thinker of all time.*

When I get home, a fundamentalist prayer circle is being held in my living room.

What does this mean, you ask?

I am a man of routine: after feeding five white mice to the boas (Garth's voice in the back of my head tells me the most enterprising snake should get a one-mouse bonus), I plan to sneak in through the bathroom window for some stealth hygiene. Such an operation consists of showering, brushing my teeth, and shaving as quietly as possible in the dark. I am highly skilled. Catlike, I plan to slip out the window again and drive to the Blossom, where I will park and sleep in the car. But today, I'm worried. There's a prayer circle in my living room where there should only be dust, vinyl, and remorse.

In a cardboard box in the trunk, I've got a bouquet of the silk flowers Beth collects, a new pink satin bathrobe (on which I paid to have a B monogrammed), a white teddy bear Jesus with a plush crown of thorns and a puffy red heart on its tummy that reads, *I forgive you because I love you!*, and a brand-new copy of *Chicken Soup for the Quilter's Soul* to bring my wife's *Chicken Soup* collection up to date; though, to my knowledge, she does not quilt. These are the peace offerings I plan to leave in conspicuous locations around the house over the course of several days.

But with ten fundamentalists in my living room, casting prayer circles and calling up Jesus from the netherworld or whatever it is they do, there's no room for plush teddys and forgiveness. They close ranks; *Chicken Soup* becomes just another demonic manifesto; and I become 100 percent sinner in everything for all time. Period. Another possibility—that they're actually in there waiting for me—means they could be some kind of Protestant Inquisition, some kind of radical Christian *Schutzstaffel*, waiting to crucify me over the fireplace with sanctified nails and eat my soul. I peer through the windshield into the big living room window for a few minutes then put the car in reverse.

Man: "What is corruption?"
Jesus: "It's you."
The Devil: "It's nothing."
Sun Tzu: "Have you looked on the other side of that
    hill?"

The hill: Rooms 144 through 168. The roaches have been uncharitably horny. It doesn't matter that we're about to unleash a boiling tide of death-spray designed to kill them all or that such chemicals will probably shorten our life spans by ten years. It doesn't matter that we work for a corrupt, coke-snorting asshole who likes to play dress up. What does matter, according to Otis, is deception:

> "All warfare is based on deception. Hence, when
> able to attack, we must seem unable; when us-
> ing our forces, we must seem inactive; when we
> are near, we must make the enemy believe we
> are far away; when far away, we must make him
> believe we are near."

Otis stands with us outside Room 144, delivering *The Art of War* as if it were a fiery Baptist sermon designed to cast out demons. He holds the text at arm's length and looks down his nose through his spectacles, gas mask pushed up on top of his head like a second face turned toward heaven.

Tomlin's got his own mask down, locked to the PVC collar of his hazmat suit. His breath comes in soft hisses. He sounds like Colorado State Birding Trail the morning I woke up on the backseat of the Caprice with its body outlining the curvature of my skull: *don't worry. Everything will be okay as soon as another mouse comes along.* I didn't have the heart to tell the snakes that I'm the one providing the mice, not some benevolent snake god in the sky. Tomlin isn't a snake or a snake god, though he sounds like a monstrous python when he breathes. And he looks like a cartoon armadillo—long snout, dual filters at the bottom of the mask suggesting flared nostrils or some kind of round baleen as if the air were a dirty ocean. Hissing, waiting, Tomlin glares at us, his thumb on the red button of his sprayer.

"Hold out baits to entice the enemy," reads Otis. "Feign disorder, and crush him."

"Yes," says Marciel, oddly sober today and excited, ready for battle.

"*Attack* him where he is unprepared. *Appear* where you are not expected."

"Yes!"

"In order to kill the enemy, our men must be roused to *anger!*"

"Yes! Yes!"

"That there may be *advantage* from *defeating* the enemy, they must have their REWARDS!"

"¡MATE A LAS CUCARACHAS!"

And with that battle cry, Marciel kicks open the door to Room 144 and opens up, screaming, with his NCC-18 B&G Sprayer, loosing a full gallon of Cypermethrin into the air. Otis and I also start screaming, running back up the hallway, trying to get our gas masks locked to our suits.

We go to the hospital to visit Marciel, who is in surprisingly stable condition after inhaling a massive amount of insecticide. In the small coppice of oaks and willows behind the pathology lab, I release Satan, Cleano, Maltodextrin, and Colorado State Birding Trail back into nature. I would have released them somewhere near the Blossom but for the fact that they are snakes. As a result of Claudia the Bear's gentle ministrations with the cars in the Blossom's parking lot, the guests are already nervous. Someone's grandma would find Satan in her coleslaw and, much like Solomon Kane, the great Puritan witch hunter, I or one of my unfortunate colleagues would be called to destroy the evil with iron and fire.

"You realize," says Otis, leaning against a tree, "that by letting them free out here, you're probably killing them. This isn't their . . ."

"Habitat," says Tomlin.

"Yeah, habitat."

I'm not listening. Everything will *not* be okay as soon as another mouse comes along. Maybe I'm the only one present who understands that. I feel sad as I watch Cleano test the air with his tongue and begin to move tentatively, carefully, under a bramble.

"Dead today. Dead tomorrow. What's the difference?" Tomlin smiles and shrugs. But, quite frankly, I am sick to death of his phony death-worship shit. Only he survived our war against the roaches unscathed, the Blossom's WMDs having blessed Otis and me with a certain lingering incontinence. More than any of us, Tomlin had been concerned for his own safety.

I turn toward him with lightning in my eyes: "Tomlin? Why don't you go blow your ass up for science, you old phony bastard?"

"You're gonna see," he screams as I make my way back

to the hospital lot. "You're gonna see as you get old! It all gets worse! Worse!"

Maybe it gets worse. Maybe it gets better. For better or worse, I go home. There are Christians again in my living room. I know they are Christians because their expressions harden when they see me. They've finished another prayer circle. I don't know what for. It must have been a long one because they all look a little drained. They're sitting around, eating potato chips. Three of them watch a sitcom on my television, laughing when they should. I notice that Lenorah is absent, still recovering, no doubt, from her little, profane adventure at our house.

The guy making my wife laugh is fortyish with a bit of a belly. Young in the face but balding, delicate wisps of blond arcing over his scalp. His smile fades when he looks at me.

"Who's this?" he asks Beth in the tone and manner of a nervous adolescent boyfriend about to snap.

Beth says nothing, looks at the carpet, stone-still.

"I live here, too," I say.

Beth looks up at me. Suddenly. Like someone switched on the wattage in her face. "No," she says, "you live in your car."

"We put your stuff in the yard," says the guy. He gives me a little knowing smile.

"These are my friends," says Beth.

A man who loses his home and his snakes in the same day is unfortunate, sayeth Sun Tzu. And if he didn't sayeth it, he should have. It's late. The Blossom café is empty. The Kitchen Staff sees that I am alone, maybe senses that something is amiss: chum in the water. They circle in the distance, letting their fins break the surface, swishing their tails.

The CNN loop doesn't show the actual execution. The volume is off. Now it's Warren Edward Ames looking out silently at the world. The news ticker runs across the bottom of the screen, informing us that the president has announced he intends to go back to school after his term is up. Then a lurid, two-second clip of the gallows, the red jumpsuit, the black bag over Ames' head.

The Kitchen Staff stares. One of them ventures closer, wipes down one of the small black tables with a dishcloth. A true blue-collar veteran. Her face is leathery, eyebrows drawn in severe arcs. She's got the forearms of a dockworker. She peers at me, curious. I'm a dangerous property. I'm plutonium. I look pretty worked over. She's not sure about me. She might be wiping tables at ground zero. When she straightens up, I see all her night shifts. I see her telling herself she's hard. The stresses of the years that put their stamp on her. She's marked by them, the way Warren Edward Ames is marked by what he's witnessed. And Tomlin by what he hasn't.

A terrible weariness sits on my heart.

I glance away. I don't want her to see that I understand her. Because if she sees my recognition and her face falls, if she drops her hostility and stops believing she's a tough, cast-iron broad, what then? At least, she's got belief working for her. She's found something, a shelter. Like Marciel with his brandy or Garth with his Blossom. I stare at my unlit cigarette, at my nails cracked with grime.

"What's wrong with you?" She's spooked, holding the dishcloth in front of her body like a protective charm. I smile and light up. But I guess my smile is odd.

"I'm not sure." I blow a puff of smoke above my head and wink at her.

Garth's voice crackles over the two-way: "The BEAR!" his precious, little squeal full of coke and dread. "The bear's in the west lot! It just mauled a Honda! DO NOT GO OUTSIDE! For the love of God. Tomlin. Otis." Garth weeps, mumbles. The signal breaks off with a beep.

The woman backs away from me, nervous, wary.

"I've seen your kind before," she says. "Crazy eyes. You smell like shit."

I shrug. Smoke leaks out from the corners of my grin.

"Fuck this." She throws the dishcloth down and runs for the kitchen.

I want to cry but I smoke my cigarette, smile, and tell myself I've got a shelter.

The Problem of Evil in Hauberk, Missouri

Miss Tomoike can't pronounce the German for money. The problem is, neither can I.

I am in love with Miss Tomoike.

I say, "*Ich habe kein Geld.*" I have no money. And the class responds, "*Wir haben kein Geld.*" We have no money. In my world, the world of German 2A, no one ever has any money. But I am still in love with Miss Tomoike.

Problems.

She is sixteen years old. I am thirty-one. It is a clichéd, old story—probably as clichéd and old as having no money. Miss Tomoike's *d*'s sound like *t*'s. If I'm not careful, mine do too: "*Wir haben kein Gelt.*"

Nein.

Nein, nein, nein.

I dance around the room for no reason at all and the class snickers. *Geld: gay-aey-elle-day.* The class repeats. They are patient, indulgent. They see my lighthearted antics and raise me my lack of correct pronunciation despite the fact that every day, at 9:10 AM in Room 22, I am barely in the game.

My feelings for Miss Tomoike endure. They torment me from her wonderfully messy homework, the lopsided *A*'s, the undotted *i*'s. I've bought a pack of the pens she uses: Pilot Precise V5 Rolling Ball, blue (extra fine). Sometimes I copy her signature over and over. I am a sad, sad man.

Jeremy Hoff raises his hand. Both of his parents are from

Augsburg, *directly* from Augsburg. He could teach my class, and he makes sure I know this every day. Jeremy Hoff is the worst thing in my life.

He reminds me: "We did this yesterday."

"Yes," I say, "yes," and retreat to the table at the front of the room where the teacher's answer book is open to the lesson I almost understand.

Jeremy laces his fingers behind his head and leans back in his desk. He's wearing Western boots. He crosses his legs straight out at the ankles and the boots make a *thok-thok* on the hardwood. "What did you do before you were a teacher?" he asks.

I tell them to open their books.

He says something in a complex Bavarian slang I don't understand, and the class snickers again. I ignore him. Miss Tomoike has beautiful eyes. Her short black hair is meticulously clean. She smiles up at me and I move on to verbs. Verbs are good. One can depend on verbs. I say, "*sprechen*," and try not to stare as she conjugates.

I took it as the innate goodness and simplicity of small-town folk that Claire Dunlop, the principal of Alexander Weiskopf High School, offered to rent me a room until I could find a place of my own. Now we have a different principal and Claire Dunlop is gone. Two years have passed, but I am a hundred years older and I think back to my arrival as if it happened in a different era. I was in the last group of teachers to live in her house on Main Street, equidistant from the gas station and the school.

Hired by Claire right out of college, I moved from California so I could teach English and wouldn't have to be a jeweler like every other member of my family. I would have gone just about anywhere. And Hauberk, Missouri, seemed okay even though tornados ripped across the state every year and the Hauberkians didn't appear to care as long as their own, personal houses still had roofs when they got home from work. Sometimes entire barns were razed, animals carried for miles, tumbleweeds, bushes, and dirt pulverized into clumps by the road or rising out of the blasted cornfields in lopsided columns—messages in the great symbolic language of creation: DON'T STAY HERE. I didn't listen.

Claire sent the algebra teacher, Henry Barber, to pick me up at the Greyhound one county over. He was a thin-lipped man, completely bald, with high cheekbones and a heaviness around him as if he traveled in his own pocket of dense air. He drove an old mint Packard in mint condition, which made me want to like him. But neither of us spoke much on the drive back to Hauberk.

Henry. What is there to say about him? He had the stick-to-itiveness of Midwestern farm culture all over him, the implicit understanding that anything worth being done was worth the time necessary to do it. Consequently, he didn't drive over forty mph and I spent most of the trip doing what I'd been doing on the bus. I watched the geometry of the fields, haystacks, distant crows fluttering up in bursts, how the sky bent into the earth at the edge of sight and seemed to get darker there, as if an end really did exist beyond which all Missouri would disappear. Winter was coming. Later that day, I'd see blue run into gray, clouds like dead chunks, clotted and falling. I'd get used to seeing the sky as a dour, unfriendly predictor: tinged green for tornados, red for heavy wind, blue for dense humidity, gray for everything else. And, like the Midwestern sky, Henry Barber's face was bland and serious, both long and compressed at the same time with a set expression and flat hazel eyes that seemed to be looking at the horizon even when they were looking at you.

"Yep, here we are, I guess," he said. His voice startled me after the long silence.

There were only eight streets in Hauberk, and I hadn't noticed that we'd come in. Though we were supposedly in the heart of the "downtown" area, it seemed like we'd entered a slightly more versatile truck stop. We got out and Henry put some quarters in an ancient parking meter.

It was the biggest house in this part of the world. If Claire Dunlop hadn't been waiting at the top of her front steps, I would have thought we'd stopped at the county courthouse. As it turned out, the courthouse was one block away on the other side of the street. And it was smaller. Henry leaned against the car and sighed. Claire was looking down from the porch, raising her arms like Christ over Rio, embracing us, the town, the sacred perfection of everything that led up to her door.

Her T-shirt is tight and pink, says *Love Kitten* over a gray cartoon cat with hearts for eyes. She hands me her Midterm Progress Report and smiles. Ice glittering on the frosted window makes a pinwheel of light on her neck. I look at it and smile back, feeling just like that gray love kitten curled up in the sun. The students press out of my classroom—all but Jeremy Hoff glaring from the door.

There are only a few reports left for me to sign. In the totalitarian world of high school, a report of "Not Satisfactory" results in the victim being sent to the school psychologist and an emergency conference with parents and teachers. A "Poor" means regular therapy, tutoring every day, and a grand jury investigation. Probably electroshock. There are no "Poor" students at Alexander Weiskopf High School.

"How are you?" asks Miss Tomoike, still smiling, beaming out ten thousand gigavolts of *Love Kitten* all over me.

I grin like a boy and mark the "Very Good" box.

"Okay," she says. "Thank you. Have a good day." A few more bonus volts before the smile disappears and she's out the door with Jeremy, who's been having a desperate power shortage—blackouts, failures, exploding circuits. He hates me, yes, but that's nothing compared to how much I hate him. I step into the hall, hands clasped behind my back, and watch them go to her locker.

Miss Tomoike's American name is Lydia. And, of all the Lydias I've known, she is the most un-Lydia, which makes me love her even more. Her real name is Aniko, but everyone must call her Lydia, the name of three of my ex-girlfriends. I am cursed by that name.

First there was Lydia MacLeod: tall, redhead, hated father, abortion at fifteen, moved to Canada then hated Canada, made me bleach my hair, left me for a bouncer.

Then there was Lydia Horton: med student, chess and bowling, eating disorder, hated father, moved to Sri Lanka to build huts for the blind.

And Lydia Rundegaard: married to textile magnate, bisexual, abstract photographer, chain smoker, hated father, broke my television.

Now I no longer own a television and Miss Tomoike doesn't bowl. She is an exchange student. Her parents live in Tokyo—bankers, businessmen, important people of commerce. I imagine sitting down with them. She'll bring me home to meet them. Finally, yes, things will work out. An unconventional match? Of course, but aren't all the great ones unconventional? I'll sit down over *awabi* and twig tea with eight-thousand-year-old Grandfather, exchanging deep existential truths in the form of short poems that seem like politeness. I'm preparing for it. I've learned three expressions from my *Japanese On One Word a Day: Gaido-san desu-ka?* Are you a guide? *Saiko sokudo hyaku kiro.* Maximum speed one hundred kilometers. *Iro, iro domo arigato.* Thank you for everything.

When Henry and I drove up, Claire Dunlop emerged in state. There was James Reid, music teacher, to her left, and Coach Spinadella on her right. She'd wrapped herself in gauzy yellow cotton, something between Cleopatra and Glenda the Good Witch of the North. And she seemed to radiate, if not beauty, then a certain conviction of her own seductiveness, trying to *flow* down her whitewashed steps but having to go very deliberately so as not to trip on the hem of her dress. This was a Claire Dunlop different from the person I'd met at the interview, sitting in the Oleander Room at the Day's Inn outside Saint Louis, where she was all polyester angles and sobriety, black coffee and the students and educational theory and what we expect. Henry, I noticed, had already become steam, blowing away so quietly I hadn't had time to thank him for the ride. So I left my bags in the Packard and met Claire's hand halfway up the steps. Everyone tried to smile.

"Would you?" she said. It was a question, but the flick of her hand toward my bags said *Go* and Spinadella went. That was the beginning. A more intelligent person would have seen past, present, and future all phenotyped at once in that gesture. A more intelligent person would have jumped back in the Packard, punched it, shot the covered wood bridge over the dry creek outside of town and been down the I-44 before any of them had a chance to say what. But I wasn't that smart and Packards don't go very fast and I was constrained by all the usual human courtesies.

It might have been the awe I felt at Spinadella's thirteen-inch biceps that made me go along. His blond hair was so clean it gleamed: the first Italian Viking. We watched him open the Packard, scoop up my suitcase and backpack in one gesture, and lumber up into the house without a word.

"We're so very, very happy you're here," said Claire, putting her arm around my shoulders and leading me up the steps, while James Reid smiled behind us like someone in her livery waiting for an order or maybe just waiting to catch her if she tripped and fell backwards.

I was amazed at the house. Safavid rugs, crystal chandeliers, authentic Victorian chic right down to cloth tubes over the chair legs. It was in the National Register of Historic Places. An antebellum plantation two-story, replete with Corinthian columns, domed pergola in the backyard, and two hundred years of whitewash—one of the few buildings left from Missouri's time as a slave state. The whole town took a certain pride in it. Carolers began there every Christmas. The Lutheran youth group whitewashed it once a year. People got married on its wide front lawn.

"We have no electricity here." She smiled with an air of confidence and secrecy that told me she could see I was down for whatever. "We preserve our traditions here just as they have always been preserved, meaning a respect for the past."

I nodded. Of course.

Claire was no stranger to history. She taught the European variety to juniors every semester. And, though she'd never been outside Missouri, her subject and her position as principal made her the local sage. In the deep, violating humidity of the Missouri summer, the mayor could often be seen conferring with her in the shade of the pergola, sipping fortified punch and hiding from the brutal realities of the political life.

She took me up the grand staircase into my room at the top. It was small and the ceiling was low, but it was very clean and white. Spinadella had left my bags on the bed. There was a washbasin and a bureau with a small round mirror, a free-standing oak closet, throw rug alongside the bed, writing table with a candelabrum, and an oversized crucifix on the wall above it. Jesus' wounds were bright and dripping. Dinner was at five. The housekeeper's name was Pattie.

After class, I go to the cafeteria for coffee and a pudding. Jorge Rodriguez-Jackson is there sucking on a toothpick, plotting, squinting into the suspect distance. He looks me over and nods. I nod back and focus on the pudding. Pudding might be one of the last good things in life. Pudding is innocent, beyond reproach. Pudding would never get you accused of making someone disappear. Nor would eating it make you want to disappear anyone. If I were Jorge Rodriguez-Jackson staring at me eating pudding, I'd know right away that I was not a disappearer. But he is not so perceptive. He blames me for Claire Dunlop's untimely vanishing act two years ago.

Jorge and his wife are from Kansas City. He teaches health and English Lit, has always taught health and English Lit, will always teach health and English Lit. I was supposed to have been hired to replace him. If anyone should be suspect for her disappearance, it should be him. Still, he blames me. He is a Marxist.

He has a Marxist righteousness, a Marxist nose for sniffing out iniquity. He has channeled Karl Marx for so long that he has come to look like him: the jowly frown, the intensity in the eyes. At the first faculty party, I wandered into his study—a veritable Marxist Bacchanalia—three complete editions of *Das Kapital* in different leathers, *Economic and Philosophical Manuscripts* leaning provocatively against a marble bookend, *Grundrisse, A Critique of Political Economy*, the whole sticky tangle in both German and English. A framed picture of Marx over the writing table. There was a Marxist tinge to everything in the house, a certain alien consciousness at work, even in his wife, who'd arch her eyebrows as if all the things she'd heard about me were coming true in front of her.

He twirls the toothpick in the corner of his mouth and looks away a split second before I look at him. Feeling him about to turn his head, I glance up at the water stain shaped like a coffee ring on the ceiling. I know he's scanning my face. The three girls at the table behind me hiss angrily about hair. The janitor over in the corner stares into his chicken soup as if it were saying something remarkable. Jorge, no doubt, is recording everything, memorizing it for some future testimony.

When I asked other faculty about his politics, they looked like I'd said something dirty. *Decent folk don't bring up things like that.* So okay. So Jorge Rodriguez-Jackson and his squinting and his contempt. He'll never stop hunting me for crimes against humanity. And if I breathe the smallest sigh for Miss Tomoike, if the smallest helpless human emotion slips out, he'll be on me—chains and culpability, scandal, perversion. I can see myself behind bars. I can see myself lynched in a field. Missouri: where the great Confederate rebels went criminal, knocking over banks, Jesse James, heads blown off, segregation, Indian slaughter. It's in the people's blood. You can see it bubbling under their skin when the proletarian in the truck next to you looks at you like you just felt up his mother. Missouri's angry. Missouri wants revenge for whatever you're about to do, and Jorge Rodriguez-Jackson's watching. I can't let myself even *think* of Miss Tomoike when he's around. He can sense a certain furtiveness in me. He'd like to put me under a harsh smoking light, ask me angry questions, write my name on the floor in chalk. He knows dirty when he sees it.

I get up to leave and he makes an inquisitive face, "Finished so soon?"

"Uh, yes, pudding, you know."

"Oh?"

"It's easy to eat."

"Is that right. Easy to eat."

I move toward the cafeteria's double doors, slowly, casually.

Days and dinners came and went, and everyone was

polite. Barber, Spinadella, Reid, and I shared the bathroom at the end of the hall with absolute maturity. We passed the salt down the table when someone wanted it and stayed off the third floor, which was Claire's.

If she was in a good mood, she'd be vampy, fluttering and quick and trying to flirt with sudden meaningful looks designed to *smolder*. If she was in a bad mood, the looks grew heavy, the dark around her eyes got that way without makeup, and a pall hung over dinner. Barber would do his steam routine. And Coach Spinadella wasn't very articulate in the first place—whether from that last stubborn Viking chromosome or from the horse-juice he'd probably done as a bodybuilder. He was Claire's barometer. If she was in a funk, then so was Spinadella. He'd beam ultra-hostile glances at everyone, like he was about to chop the table in half, then eat another spoon of peas.

Only Reid kept a cheerful face no matter what. Claire would have a mausoleum death spell hanging over the table, and Reid would be shoveling food into his mouth as if he'd just been paroled, saying, "Hey, anybody watching the Chiefs tonight?"

Nobody was even if they were.

At first, I took it as passive resistance, aggressive cheerfulness. Then it seemed that Reid was inherently happy—one of those rare individuals at peace with himself and his life. But, ultimately, I understood that he was just plain insensitive. He didn't focus on anything beyond himself and so was completely content. James Reid remains for me, at least in this sense, one of history's unacknowledged geniuses.

School started and I began to teach freshman and sophomore English under the supervision of Jorge Rodriguez-Jackson, who sat at the back of my room every day to make sure I was using his lesson plans. Assignments full of nutritious Marxism that I, with my degraded bourgeois ideology . . .

Question: *How does Kent's vehemence towards Oswald in Act II, Scene ii, help portray Oswald as a capitalist prototype?* (Skipped in favor of *What kind of a guy do you think Lear is?*)

Question: *How does personification of The Red Death symbolize the embodiment of false consciousness and the effects of aristocratic exclusivity?* (Skipped in favor of *Describe the big moment in the story.*)

Question: *How does the willingness of the indigenous Africans to be exploited by Kurtz reflect the function(s) of an internalized ideological state apparatus?* (Skipped in favor of *Did you like* Heart of Darkness?)

The revolution was put down in all of my classes. Satanic capitalist ideology prevailed despite baleful looks from the political officer at the back of the room. I imagined Jorge Rodriguez-Jackson's Health 2 students marching through the quad in olive uniforms, his AP English Politburo lecturing their parents after grace about the opiate of the masses.

Still, at first, things seemed okay, seemed doable until the heavens opened up on my head. I was two weeks into my first semester at Alexander Weiskopf when it hit. It came on like one of the local twisters I'd heard about, the kind where you're supposed to jump in the bathtub and hold a mattress over your head while cows from the next county are hurtling through the air. A death in the faculty. No one to teach German. Horror. And I was the only one who could fix it. Could I substitute maybe? Could I teach a few lessons until they found someone else? It wouldn't be hard. I'd had a few years as an undergraduate. Sure, of course, I wanted to get along. Old Mr. Jürgen—who lived with his mother thirty miles outside town and spoke only *Hochdeutsch*, who'd been learning English his whole life and never quite got it down so that it pained him to speak it—had choked on phlegm and left me alone with his *Kulturspiegel*, his *Arbeitsplan*, and his fifty students, each secretly suspecting what I knew to be true: I was *planlos*, without plan. I was *cluelos*.

Later, I'd come to believe Claire had hired me just for this, that she'd foreseen it. There was no bathtub to shield me from the twister. There was no mattress. The winds had picked me up with the livestock and dropped me in Germany.

And everything took on sinister proportions. The vicious underbelly of Claire's flirtiness: was I expected to flirt back? If I did, would she let me return to just teaching English? I had one hundred and fifteen dollars in the bank, enough for a one-way ticket to nowhere. My family back in Los Angeles had disowned me: two generations of angry jewelers with no faith in education. Grandpa Gordon had been an anarchist. Dad left when I was twelve. Draft dodgers. Vehement, Nonconforming Welshmen with an uncle still doing time in Mount Joy for polygamy. They'd laugh me into the street. I had nothing to go back to.

"What do you mean by 'big moment'?" asked one of my brighter sophomores.

The problem with Pandora wasn't her curiosity as most people think. It was that Zeus gave her the box in the first place. Come on, people, let's have a little sensitivity for the Pandoras of the world. I'm thinking this—meditating on it, sympathizing with all the misunderstood little destroyers of creation—on the corner of Main and Shelly, staring into the Main Street Diner, while beside me James Reid squeaks bad saxophone at the falling snow. Reid was originally a drummer not a sax player. And, even though he teaches everything from horns to strings, drums are the only things he can play correctly.

My feet are damp. Reid has enough air in his lungs to kill everything within a six-block radius. And I'll count myself lucky if the next time he squeaks up that B-flat it'll disconnect my heart, blast me to a pile of dust, scatter my molecules into gray gutter snow. Make it quick and make it final. But that would be too easy. Tonight, my very own Pandora is on a dream date with Jeremy Hoff, and I'm destined to watch.

Yeah. Didn't Norman Rockwell paint something like this? Johnny and Jenny sharing a malt in a brightly lit diner while fluffy snowflakes glide down outside and God is in his heaven and all is right with the world? Norman never painted me. I'm freezing and I still can't figure out how Reid can play in these conditions.

He stops for a blessed moment to say, "Hey there, are

you asleep?" And then his Chic Corea version of "God Rest Ye Merry Gentlemen" starts up again like large pieces of metal crumpling into each other. Jazz, dig?

It's my job to scoop snow out of the taupe fedora on the sidewalk in front of us. James does this two nights a month for pocket money, but this is the first time I've helped him. Usually, it's his sister scooping snow out of the fedora, but she has pneumonia. He's in his forties but looks about seventy-eight—stooped, wrinkled, completely gray. It's a Friday night. Our students walk by, bored in Hauberk's tiny downtown, on their way no doubt to drunken naked pleasures neither James Reid nor I will ever know. They drop a few pity-dollars in the hat when they pass, faces blank, embarrassed for us.

Dreamy: let's have a cultural exchange. Jeremy Hoff can be second-generation German-American corn-fed Romeo from the heart of the heart of the country. And Miss Tomoike can be happy optimistic Asian beauty, who cares about the environment and wants everyone to live well. Together, they'll be a force so powerful it will blow the glass of the diner into the street, rip the space-time continuum, end reality as we know it—true enlightenment, no more pain and suffering, human evolution advanced to the next stage because of this most sacred and perfect union, amen.

Only that's not happening, is it?

Jeremy Hoff's putting his high school moves on her as only an adolescent lizard like he can. Pure reptile: the sort of seduction that makes young girls think it's true love forever. It'll never be true love. Lizards don't fall in love. It's a constitutional fact. And it's never been Pandora's fault. All Zeus: the prototype, the lying, cheating, seducing sky-lizard.

Maybe Jeremy got "hurt" a little in the past. He looks down, smiles. He's shy but he might let his "true feelings" show through his "confidence" because Miss Tomoike and he "really click" and they've got, like, "something special." I realize I've walked forward and am standing in the middle of Main, staring at them in their window seat. Ah, acid jealousy, burn, work your evil.

Reid stops playing. "What are you doing? My hat's full of snow."

Of course, there's a job to be done. When I clean the hat out, there's a dollar fifty in it. I slip the money into his trench coat and walk up the street towards my car.

"Hey," he yells. "Wait. Where you goin'?"

Good question.

My bad situation couldn't have been more perfect for Claire, who drifted through the rooms at night like a wraith. She could be as eccentric as she wanted in the House for Orphaned Teachers. Claire never slept and neither did I, hours of stay-ahead German in my brain like a nightly violation. I'd be heating a pan of water in the kitchen for my midnight don't-worry-everything's-going-to-be-okay tea and I'd see her drift soundlessly through the next room, stopping briefly to touch something on an end table or run her fingers along the curtains.

I'd ask myself whether she meant for me to see her. Was it all part of some preternatural courting ritual for high school faculty? Was Reid involved? Spinadella? Barber? Was I paranoid or had the deciding factor in hiring me been that I'd have nowhere to run? Today, German. Tomorrow, physics, calculus, organic chemistry. I could see my future forming in all its nasty glory. She could make me do anything. And what would I be able to do about it? Just nod and start reading the textbooks. After the rent deduction, there was no way for me to afford utilities and pay Claire for my portion of the dinner budget. I already owed her. If I ran, I knew she'd send Spinadella to collect.

He was the perfect leg-breaker. Spinadella and his linemen regularly growled at the top of their lungs in the tiny weight room attached to the gym. They'd scream out blood-death calls in some language invented by the Frankensteins, Albertus Magnuses, Doctor Moreaus of the world—master-mind handlers who knew how to control the beasts. But now the creatures were loose and in high school, free to shave their heads and pump as much iron as they wanted, free to flex their way through any class—untouchable, terrifying, and hog-dumb. They stood at least a foot taller than the other students and had the same slow contempt for other life forms that one has for ants trying desperately to avoid the shoe.

Their shrieks and grunts played out in echoes over the quad, knocking between the buildings as if the linebackers had mated, multiplied, and had finally broken their cage locks. Free at last. Fresh meat. Like their coach, they always seemed to be wavering on the edge of a steroid berserk. Teachers passed them partly out of pressure to keep the football team intact, partly out of self-preservation. Françoise, the bulimic French instructor from Lyons, would run to the bathroom and vomit after first period—not for her usual bulimic reasons but because she was shaking from fear. Unnamed persons had once held her upside down and pinched her nose shut while she counted backwards from *cent*.

I should have felt lucky not to have gotten any of them in German. But I would have gladly vomited every day in exchange for not having to live with Spinadella, who'd openly stare at me like he wanted to kill me. On the surface, he respected my personal space, a clear-cut DMZ that he wouldn't violate. But there were stray shots: the hard looks, the collision in the hall that left a baseball-sized bruise above my bottom rib. I didn't know what he had against me. I went over everything, searching for a slight, a stupid joke, an off-color word skewed to an insult when I wasn't looking. But, of course, I had no idea. I avoided him in the cafeteria, made no eye contact at dinner, kept to myself, afraid for my life.

Borges' parable: Dante, exiled in Ravenna, dreams of a tiger dreaming in a cage below the Coliseum and then realizes that he is dreaming about himself. He is the tiger; Ravenna is the cage. He and the tiger share a blessed unity in the dream-state. I wonder why I haven't had a similar dream. All the greats had a guiding star—Constantine's floating cross, Hemingway's bull fights, Blake's demons giggling in his shop. I have nothing but Miss Tomoike.

Looking through black branches at her studying on her bed, I realize that this parable stinks: alone in the darkness under a dead maple tree, the pathetic exile nurses a broken heart without the luxury of tigers. And in the end—every parable needs a twist—is he redeemed? Is he relieved? Or does he wake up in Ravenna?

She's not looking out the window. And, if she did, what would she expect to see? Twenty squares of beveled darkness. People don't bother curtaining their windows because Hauberk has never had a peeper. Not until now. I walk up and press my palms against the warm glass. My breath makes crystals on the pane before interior heat turns them to droplets that freeze half-way down.

A strand of her hair is caught in the corner of her mouth. She's wearing black overalls and a T-shirt. I can't tell what she's reading. It's not German. Good for her. Miss Tomoike's English is so good that she can take German in America; she's brilliant. The glass is warm, comforting in the cold like touching a living thing.

How could someone so beautiful and intelligent fall in love with a kid like Jeremy Hoff? It's the question I'd really like to ask. If I were her father, I'd ask it. If I were her friend. Anyone but me. Nothing to do but spread my palms on the glass and ask myself: how could she?

I walk away slowly, pulling a branch off the maple tree with a hard crack. I don't care if she looks out. Let her see me swinging gashes in the snow, splintering the branch against a wooden post. My hands are cold and I don't feel the splinters, cutting diagonally across a hard-packed snowfield, hitting any lump or post until I'm holding a wooden fragment. I'll bet Miss Tomoike didn't even get up. If she did, she didn't think of me. She saw part of a handprint, the residue of breath, and thought of Jeremy Hoff or maybe thought of nothing, not so brilliant after all.

The sight of a distant car, however, gives me pause. It's Jorge Rodriguez-Jackson's brown Škoda. How many other people in Hauberk drive a brown Škoda? I walk straight towards it, but it takes off before I can make out who the driver is through the new snowfall. I tell myself I am not an offender. I repeat.

Claire had been leaning in the doorway to my room, staring at me. I was studying. The German had blunted my senses and I'd forgotten the door ajar.

"Yes?" I cleared my throat and made an unintimidated face.

Her eyes flicked to the cross-shaped bright spot on the wall above my desk where the crucifix was supposed to be. Every night, I took it down and hid it because Jesus' gaze would follow me in the flickering candlelight. Every day, the housekeeper would find it and put it back. In the interview, Claire had asked if I was a Lutheran. I told her I'd been a devout Lutheran my whole life, making a mental note to learn what that was. And now she'd caught me, but Claire only smiled. She was in her nightgown.

"Just looking at you." Her voice was even-toned, but I could see a distant, glazed look in her eyes. Had she just taken her medication or did she need some? The door closed. The nightgown came off. Claire's body was shaped like a large white thumb. She walked to the bed and looked at me.

"Get over here," she said.

I closed my notebook and quietly laid my pen down on the desk. I felt detached; the sight of Claire's body had shocked me into some basic motor-survival mode. I thought I might go downstairs and take a walk. The fact that I was in my pajamas and slippers did not occur to me. When I opened the door, Spinadella glared at me from the end of the hall, all bulging six-three, two hundred and fifty pounds of him.

I thought of my job and of how the one hundred and fifteen dollars I had wouldn't cover a new set of teeth. Claire was waiting behind me, hands on hips, mouth in a tight knowing smile. She grabbed my crotch and backed me onto the bed.

"Tell me you love me," she said.

The word for the day is *Gewissensbisse*. The phrase for the day is *Gewissensbisse haben*: remorse, to have remorse, to feel remorseful.

Here's Miss Tomoike with her big brown eyes.

Her midterm looks like an execution. I emptied the red pen. Invented new criticisms on the spot. Large heaps of teacherly lash. And for what? Vengeance. If I could have nailed Jeremy Hoff, I would have, but his work is untouchably good.

Deep, in the inner darkness of my being, I have sometimes prayed for him to fail an assignment. Yes, a cardinal sin— paradise lost, lake of fire, burning, gnashing of teeth, no teacher heaven when I die.

She's the last student left in the room. She's trying not to break down. I half sit on the table up front, just like an adult, waiting, as if to say, *That's life, honey.* And the sad thing is I'm right. *There are a lot of pathetic, vindictive, lonely people out there, Miss Tomoike (can I call you Lydia?), and you just got yourself one.*

"I tried . . . hard." Pristine, angelic teardrop down cheek.

"I know," I say. "I understand."

Now she's weeping. She's letting it all out. Sobs. Even a few wails, moans. Miss Tomoike looks down at her paper as if she still can't believe it. Actually, it's not that bad. I don't tell her that after seeing her on a date with Jeremy Hoff my standards for her work went up 500 percent. And the part of me that wants to burn down the children's hospital, spray the petting zoo with toxic waste, see all privileged sniffling little flowers broken under boots—that part is completely satisfied. That's right: *suffer, suffer, suffer.*

"Am I going to fail? Is there anything I can do?" The skin under her eyes is extra red where she's viciously attacked her tears with the sleeve of her sweater. Miss Tomoike hates her tears. She sits very straight in her desk.

"Of course, there's always something you can do. Failure is pretty far off, I think, if you want to put out some extra effort."

"Yes." Smiling, nodding, wiping her eyes.

"Why don't you meet me here after school tomorrow and we'll go through your paper, maybe talk about rewriting it." That's reasonable, isn't it? She thinks so. I picture what she'll be wearing tomorrow after school and smile benevolently.

Miss Tomoike is now incredibly happy: good people do exist, forgiveness is a beautiful thing. Teacher wants you to learn. He'll correct your faults. She thanks me profusely, but I wave it off. "Don't mention it," I say and watch Love Kitten No. 1 walk out of my room.

I tried to laugh it off, but I didn't have any more energy. I'd been too accommodating. I'd hesitated, there, in the kitchen, watching her drift through the rooms. Was it the hesitation? How does a man put this into words? We have no language for it.

After a while, Claire no longer needed the threat of Spinadella to force me into it. She had her own key and entered at night. We never talked. Her nightgown came off and my body did what it did while my mind was on a beach in California, contemplating the waves or how wind takes root in the palms and seems to live there for a time. In the morning, I'd stare at the dark ceiling over my bed and think: *why did I have to wake up?* I'd think: *there must be a logic to this.* I've always believed there's a logic to everything.

Tired. Days muted to their lowest setting. I'd walk through the halls and look at the students as if they were fish in an aquarium. When had all adolescents begun to look exactly the same—drifting down the halls in groups, quietly glassed-off from existence, unaware of anything beyond themselves? Had they always been like this? And my life too: a different kind of fish but equally distant or maybe just an empty tank thrown open to the sun—yellow-green depth, sediment lit from above, where you might stop to wait for a fish and, when it didn't appear, feel ridiculous for staring into empty water.

Claire owned me. What objection could I make that anyone would take seriously? What hold did she have on Spinadella, on Reid and Barber? No one talked about it. There was no resistance, no underground railroad, no solidarity. I looked for a sign, a bent word, a wink, any kind of acknowledgment, code tapped on the pipes at night. But nothing. Dinner remained dinner, light pitter-patter, long protracted silences. Claire would be having an up day or a down day. Reid would be gently oblivious, Barber impersonating a distant cloud formation, and Spinadella beaming out hostility like hell's only lighthouse. With my inner volume turned down, I had nothing to say. I was the Quiet One. It was all I could do to keep the candelabrum lit on my desk at night after hiding the crucifix someplace new.

I never heard steps on the thick rugs, but her weight made the floorboards creak. In the middle of the night, I'd listen to Claire pace and stop, pace and stop for hours, and sometimes, a much heavier person—Spinadella—faint dance hall music from the thirties filtering down through the wood. The thought of them dancing above me seemed terrifying and obtuse the way the reenactment of a battle leaves corpses in the landscape that aren't dead. Undead. One word and the corpses stand up grinning, a pantomime of life.

Love maketh men do strange things, Horatio.

The day is all anticipation. Am I too pale? Is the gut showing? Is my hair out of whack? It feels like prom. I never went to prom, spending the night instead on the roof of the Imperial Toy Company in downtown LA, reading Camus, hoping that the girl I'd casually mentioned it to would find me mysterious enough to follow. She never showed up. I went home when it started to rain.

But Miss Tomoike, she'll be here. Seduction of the innocent. The predator doesn't worry about the baby giraffe. If he did, how would he eat? There's no blame in nature, no blame when you're starving for some giraffe. *Come not betwixt the dragon and his wrath*, says Lear. That's right. Come not. And if you do come, well, that's fate isn't it.

I go to the men's room between classes and stare at my face in the mirror. I don't look like the dragon and his wrath. More like the baby giraffe. Not even that good. Sallow. Sunken eyes. Wrinkles around the mouth. More like the aging Komodo dragon. At thirty-one, I'm already a half-gray, wrinkled, German-teaching Komodo. It's ridiculous to think I could seduce her. But here I am.

Miss Tomoike's class is its old ugly self. Twenty-five separate shades of contempt looking back at me. Jeremy Hoff's work, no doubt. The phrase list we're on deals with a trip to the dentist. I say X and the students answer Y. It's not supposed to be hard.

Ist es ein Abszeß? Is it an abscess? I manage to pronounce the sentence pretty well, I think, but a wave of sniggering goes around the room.

Ja, they answer, *es ist ein Abszeß.*

Jeremy Hoff is participating today, still riding the glory of having thrown the winning pass against Rigg County last night. He and Miss Tomoike exchange glances when they think I'm not looking.

Können Sie mir eine Spritze geben? Can you give me anesthetic?

Nein, they say, *nein, wir haben keine Spritze.* We have no anesthetic.

Ich kann nicht schlafen. I can't sleep.

Ja, they answer. No more sniggering.

Ich kann nicht essen. I can't eat.

Ja. Some of the students nod or look away.

Ich habe Schmerzen. I'm in pain.

No one says anything. Maybe it's my tone.

"Come on." I grip the edges of the table, lean towards them. *Wiederholen Sie.* Repeat.

The clock's broken hands spasm and click. *Wir haben Schmerzen*, Jeremy says.

We look at each other.

Outside, the sophomore girls are shrieking by their lockers. A boy is laughing the long, high mean-spirited laugh of the adolescent. The kind of laugh that comes with pointing, that's serrated, that leaves one bleeding, with an *Abszeß*, in need of immediate attention. Someone at the back of the room coughs. I look down at the last phrase on the list.

Wieviel bin ich Ihnen schuldig? I ask. How much do I owe?

Claire's sudden disappearance, when it came, had far less tragedy for those of us who lived with her every day than for greater Hauberk, suddenly buzzing with the hint of scandal. I wasn't going to miss her.

They found her clothes laid out on a chair. Everything up on the third floor was as it had always been, Victorian tea furniture unbroken, crystal figurines of ballet dancers perfectly arranged in their wall case, her gigantic lace doilies unrumpled, no psychopathic messages in lipstick on her gilded bathroom mirror, no bloody prints in the porcelain tub. Nothing. Just poof and gone. Claire's British history class had been the last to see her. According to them, there had been nothing exceptional in her behavior that day. God save the Queen.

Dinner on that first Claireless night had been awkward. Very little was said. We were stunned. It was the first dinner Claire had ever missed. And, for many dinners after, we would still be unsure what to say to each other. We'd become like medieval prisoners blinking suddenly into daylight, our new liberty glaring and unwieldy.

The sheriff came sniffing around as sheriffs are supposed to, but he didn't sniff too vigorously. The farmland outside Hauberk was searched. The house's basement was dug up and found to be no dirtier than dirt. There were no newly cultivated mounds in the backyard. No telling piles of ash and fillings in the snowfield behind the graveyard. In short, she'd left the earth without a trace. And I felt like dancing a moonlight samba. I felt like having cases of burgundy delivered to all inbred schizophrenic killers hiding in barn lofts for a hundred miles. At night, I heard the patter of little feet—my own. I was even dancing in my sleep.

Of course, there was Jorge Rodriguez-Jackson: all suspicion, that toothpick in the corner of his mouth. But the life of Hauberk, Missouri, continued. People got tired of speculating, inventing theories. The paper stopped running her picture. A tornado had taken out a village to the east. Drought was expected that summer. A graduate student at the University of Missouri had committed suicide. These things were news, not Claire's disappearance, which became uninteresting and thus faded out of the collective consciousness as if it had never happened.

Hulking Spinadella, at least for me, was the prime suspect. But he went crazy on one of his halfbacks during a scrimmage and crippled the boy with his fists. He's still in jail. Reid moved in with his sister and I found my cottage outside town. Only Barber remained. Claire had willed the house to the mayor, who became the new landlord, and the space suited Henry just fine. I dropped by to visit him a few months later, but he didn't ask me in. We stood on the porch and stared into the darkened Jiffy Lube across the street. He kept his hands in his pockets, and I could see that the solitude had not made him any more pleasant.

"Well," he said, "I guess she's gone."

"Guess so."

"I guess you'll miss her."

I looked at him, but he was staring into Jiffy Lube like he might learn something important if only he didn't blink. We listened to the night. Crickets were chirping somewhere far away, somewhere I wanted to be.

"Henry?"

"Yeah?"

"Fuck off, okay?"

If there's a time I can meet with you off campus, maybe, with just a little more help, instruction, tutoring, supervision thinks the old Komodo. But her midterm sits on the table between us like a chessboard, and what was so simple in my fantasies seems byzantine now. Checkmate in three? I don't think so. Miss Tomoike's arms are crossed. She's looking down, her aura dark. What did I expect? She's assimilating. Ten minutes ago, like a loose American girl, she was kissing Jeremy Hoff by his locker and then they walked, hand in hand, toward my room—slowly, as if one of them were about to be executed. "I'll be right outside," he said too loudly. Her protector.

We sit in silence for a few moments, both of us staring at her exam. I imagine Jeremy in the hall listening, his ear to my door. In a samurai film, I would hear his heartbeat, firing arrow suddenly through paper partition into chest of interloping spy. Just so. Impudent Romeo dispatched with alacrity by old arrow-shooting Komodo.

She uncrosses her arms and I notice her fingers are stained with ink. She's been writing: love notes to Jeremy, letters of discontent to Tokyo. Japanese in ballpoint, such a waste. One requires a brush, a straight back, high virgin-white vellum that takes the ink like a momentous event. The paper loses a certain innocence but gains the character of the writing, bringing the female-yin-black letters together with the male-yang-white sheet—the unification of all duality. That's the sort of writing instruction I've had in mind for Miss Tomoike (segue to Confucius: "It furthers one to undertake an affair with an older man. No blame."). More likely: *Mother, Father, the teachers here are horrible. There is this one monster in particular. He looks like a lizard.*

"I'm sorry, but could you tell me how this is wrong?" Tentative, polite, sincerely worried, but with an undercurrent. Resentment? No. Coaching. I can hear Jeremy telling her to question me, telling her I don't know what I'm talking about. The truth is that her answers are fine. The questions were short-answer, interpretive. I look at my red Xs, where I pressed so hard the pen left furrows in the page, and feel ridiculous.

"Well," I say, "the questions were pretty open ended."

She nods, her expression blank.

"And there's a certain degree of subjectivity . . ."

"I don't understand." More forcefully now. Jeremy Hoff in ballpoint all over her. All she's missing is his regulation sneer. The truth is that her answers are probably better than what I might have written. The truth is that I'm an apprentice molester and Confucius was Chinese.

Bright hot reality: Miss Tomoike is a child. *Love Kitten* doesn't even factor in. I'm horrified at the sudden clear vision of myself as Claire. I hear Jeremy clear his throat loudly outside my door.

"The truth is, Miss Tomoike, I've called you here to tell you that I've re-evaluated your work. I'm changing your grade."

A thousand thank yous. She doesn't ask why. And she's out the door before I can find the inner pulleys that make my face smile. The Christmas cologne I never wear sickens me. I go to the window and stare out over a runny snowfield at my home—the worthless, never-ending latitude of Missouri.

All this happens. The snow has melted and the news says there's a tornado coming. But I don't know. There's always a tornado coming. Shadows are indistinct. The day begins dark and never truly gets light, while the ghost of old Mr. Jürgen wanders the state, trying to explain itself in correct English. I laugh, but who can say why a tornado takes one house and leaves another. Just get in the bathtub. Maybe Claire Dunlop is living a quiet life on the Santa Monica strand with a husband and a tight pink T-shirt that reads *Love Kitten*. Maybe Jorge Rodriguez-Jackson has a file on me waiting for the FBI. Maybe right now Miss Aniko Lydia Tomoike is breaking all available speed laws, jumping snowbanks in a Husq Varna Motorized 2023 Ice Sled, headed here with apologies, justifications, words of love and eternity. It wouldn't surprise me. Odds are garbage. Opinions are meaningless. Everything happens. It's all here.

Ghost Town

Dogs cannot be made to look like human beings. You're sitting on the rooftop deck at Dick's Chop House in Fresno, California, and this is one thing you know. There is nothing modern science can do to make a dog resemble a person. The waitress comes and goes. Dennis lights a cigarette, leans back in his chair, and watches moths flit around pale yellow deck lights.

"Look," you say. "It's here: 'Federal Scientific Panel Tests Limits of Cosmetic Surgery on Dogs.'"

Dennis coughs against the back of his hand. "Want to hear the one about how a dog both does and does not wag its tail at the same time?"

These trips to Fresno are making you nervous. Brown smears of pollution hang over searing afternoons. Police are everywhere. Fistfights on sidewalks. Porcelain statues of saints and shrines to dead relatives on porches. Car shows in parking lots. SUVs with rims and tint jobs bouncing high at the stoplights. From Dick's roof, you can see Blackstone Avenue three stories below, stinking, pulsing, clotted with angry traffic at nine on a Friday night. Flashing lights in the distance. Always. Bassed-up mariachis from passing lowriders make your empty beer bottle vibrate on the patio table.

"I can't shake the feeling we're about to get shot," you say.

Dennis looks at you for a moment and then holds up

his cigarette, watches smoke uncoil from the tip. "Relax. Dogs can tell when they're being filmed. Know that?"

You scan the rest of the front page. Murder. Lies. Bombing. Abductions.

"You can't just film dogs when nobody's around to see if they'll wag their tails," he says. "They *always* know you're watching."

You try to remember if you asked the waitress to bring another beer. You tell Dennis you can't understand why someone funded a government project to see if dogs could look like people. You cross and re-cross your boots at the ankles, light one of his cigarettes, and think about the future. It's been fifteen minutes since Warren went downstairs to meet the buyer. In about fifteen more, you will finally have enough money to live comfortably for at least a year or be arrested.

The waitress brings two more beers. Black hair, thin, pretty, she looks barely twenty-one. Dennis tips her a dollar, and she rolls her eyes. He smiles and watches her go.

It's the tree in the forest thing," he says. "First, you take a dog and put it in a room. Inside the room you have a bunch of nuclear waste. If the waste gives off too much radiation, a machine detects it and smashes a can of nerve gas. But if you look straight at the door of the room, there's no way to tell if the machine has smashed the can or not."

You imagine a plastic surgeon's scalpel cutting into the muzzle of a screaming Golden Retriever and shake the thought away, drink your beer. A police copter hovers over distant city lights. Its searchlight probes like a glowing feeler.

"Which means you can't tell if the dog is alive or dead," Dennis adds.

"And that's why you can't tell if it's wagging its tail?"

"No." Dennis pauses, takes another drag, and looks at you a bit longer this time. "This is a hypothetical example. The tail comes in a minute."

Five trips from San Diego to Fresno in as many months. And each time, you carried enough illegal items to stop your happy thoughts for a good, long time if you got caught. An hour ago, you parked stolen truck number five in the lot behind Dick's. It's loaded with one hundred and seventy-eight cases of premium vodka that should have been in Reno, according to the bill of lading. Stealing interstate means federal time. A possibly dead driver means life. You smoke Dennis's cigarette and try not to think about it. Instead, you read yesterday's paper filled with all the heinous shit people already got caught for.

"So the fucking dog is now in a *quantum state*. It's both alive and dead until you open the door. Maybe it's wagging its tail. Maybe it's just a stiff little bundle of joy."

"But wait. You can never find out because if you open the door you might get nerve-gassed. You can't risk opening the door."

"Fuck that," says Dennis. "You've got a spacesuit. That's not the point."

Then it doesn't matter because Warren walks up to the table with a grin. "All done." He takes a long drink of your beer. "Andre says we're good. We go out back right now and get paid."

"Fucking-A," you say, standing up. Dennis stands, too.

The waitress walks out onto the deck, sees Dennis, Warren, and you grinning at each other, and takes a step back. "What?" she says.

"Dogs," says Dennis. "We like dogs."

She looks at the three of you and nods slowly.

You wink.

Andre is an extremely large, extremely stupid man dressed like a farmer in a plaid shirt and overalls. He's got a shaved head with a dark red birthmark shaped like Florida on the back. Every time you have to deal with Andre, you wonder what he would do if he lived in Florida and people kept asking him why the state was tattooed on his head. He'd likely kill a few of the slower people and then spend the rest of his life in prison. Prison. Something not to think about when standing in a parking lot beside a sixteen-wheeler full of highjacked vodka. Andre's holding a can of Miller and doesn't seem at all bothered by passing sirens on Blackstone Avenue.

He does look like he enjoys eating chops at Dick's Chop

House. That's another thing you feel confident about besides
the bit about dogs not looking like people. The question is: if
you put the contents of Andre's belly in a quantum state—i.e.,
with or without a chop—would that mean he'd be digesting
and not-digesting at the same time? Would it mean he'd be
simultaneously hungry and not-hungry? Andre's eyes are
very small. He gives you a glazed, faintly hostile look.

"So it's all there," says Warren.

"So it is." Andre's eyes shift to his beer.

You look at Andre, at Warren, at Dennis standing
back a few feet, puffing his cigarette down to the filter, and
wonder what's going on. Usually it's Andre with a bag of
bills and then good-bye, done. Not the current Andre with the
beady expression of some fat, hostile marsupial in overalls.
Marsupials. Koalas and shit. They eat bamboo, not chops.

"Thing is," says Andre, "Jimbo don't come down no
more. He don't like being recognized. You gotta drive it over
to Madera. That's where the money is."

"What the fuck," says Warren. He's tall. Medium build.
Sandy blond hair parted on the side. Warren wants to get
mad, get up in Andre's face. But Warren doesn't get anything
more than smart. "This is bullshit," he says to the asphalt. He
puts his hands in the pockets of his Pepsi windbreaker and
looks down like a schoolboy.

Maybe Dennis could do something. He's wiry but
strong. You've seen him get in fights, get crazy, punch holes
in walls. Once, he beat the hood of his ex-wife's Firebird until
his fists were all torn up. In the morning, the car looked like
Dennis had won. But what's there to do if you want to get
paid?

Andre blinks. "Madera," he says and drains his beer.

Madera will be a challenge. Only twenty minutes
north, but getting there will be difficult. It's Memorial Day
weekend, and the police are out *en masse*, the Force in force,
making people walk the line and count back in sevens from
a hundred. There's a sobriety checkpoint every five blocks.
Driving north into Fresno earlier, you saw Highway 99 lit by
flashing lights, the first unlucky drunks of the night standing

pale and uneasy in patrol car floods. So the three of you decide to call it a night and go out to the warehouse tomorrow noon. Dennis tells Andre. Andre will call Jimbo, and all will be right with the world.

For you—for obvious reasons—traceable cell phones are a no-no. You stare at the truck and dial your girlfriend, Christina, from a filthy phone booth in the dirt lot behind the Apache Motel. You parked the truck a few feet away, right next to the room you'll share with Warren and Dennis. It looks like any other semi parked for the night, but the shadows in the cab remind you of a ghost town.

Your girlfriend's roommates call her Tina. You call her Chris. You both call your little boy Jessup because that was your grandfather's name and neither of you wanted a son named Jesse. Jesses go to jail; Jessups go to college, according to Chris, and you have no cause to disagree. But you wonder if someday he'll wear a jean jacket and a mullet, if he'll ride a motorcycle he calls a "dirt bike" and phone you from jail in the middle of the night like you did to your father. When that happens, you'll feel as sad as your father once looked standing on the other side of shatterproof glass at County, his failure complete.

Images of Dennis throwing a crowbar away from the highway. It was easy for him to whack the driver in the back of the head while Warren pointed a .45 in the guy's face. Dennis and Warren didn't like doing it that way. Neither did you. But highjacking trucks is what it is. Unless you want to spend the rest of your pathetic life in prison, it's you or the driver, who should have known what he was risking when he took the job. You listen to the connection beep and tell yourself you're a survivor. You try not to remember the groans or the sound the driver's body made when you and Warren heaved him into a ditch in the darkness.

The connection goes *beep-beep* and the answering machine comes on, Chris and Jessup together, sounding happy, laughing, saying *after the beep!* You don't mention anything about what you're doing. You hesitate and say, "Hi, Chris. Hi Jess. It's me. I miss you!"

Whenever she asks where you've been, you tell her

a story. You say that you're a dealer in dry goods, that you work for a trucking company, that sometimes you sell ladies' hats out of boxes because it's easier that way. You tell her you only sell high-end jewelry and only when you can get a good deal on it. You tell her you once owned a Zamboni that used to belong to the LA Kings, and that the price of shoes in Cleveland is much lower. Which, you add, is how you came into fifty-seven crates of Louis Vuitton Vienna Minimalisa High Boots in ostrich leather. You tell her there's nothing better than family and not to ask where the money comes from because every dollar means *I love you.* You tell her to wait, to be patient, because you're going to get her a house in a neighborhood not as violent. You tell her to be realistic because you are. You tell her you're a hustler because, in this goddamn world, everybody is. And, most of the time, you feel you're telling the truth.

"I'll be back soon," you say and wonder who's standing beside the phone listening, maybe one of Chris' cruel roommates, a blood-red nail hovering over ERASE.

"Tell Jessup I got him a present."

Ghost town: the darkened windows of the truck are like the dead spaces of abandoned buildings at night, somewhere you wouldn't want to go. After dark, they're just void, negative space. The truck cab is empty. And, you think: twenty-five years to life for interstate highjacking and maybe an accessory to murder. You think: maybe what you tell Chris isn't *the* truth; it's just *your* truth. But that doesn't make the Zamboni any less real or the fact that it came into your possession something false. You tell yourself no other thief in the world has successfully stolen and resold a Zamboni. That, too, is part of your story, your truth. Maybe, if you're lucky, the bad karma of your thieving life will take a long time to kick in, unlike with your father. Maybe then you'll know what is or is not absolutely true. Until then, you'll keep calling from dirty phone booths outside ghost towns in the dark.

"I love you both," you say. And the phone booth is silent. On its two-story pole beside the highway, the Apache Motel sign is a pale yellow circle with hot pink *Vacancy* across the center. But behind the L-shaped motel, the empty dirt lot continues into darkness. The motel is two exits up the ninety-nine from Fresno, a place Dennis says nobody cares about, where he's stayed a couple times before. When you turn your back to the highway, the empty motel, and the truck, you look across the flat dirt and feel you've reached the end of something. After this, somewhere out there in the night, there may only be emptiness and the good chance of falling into it—or maybe twenty-five years to life, waiting patiently to pounce. You're thirty-four years old. You've spent four of those years in Corcoran State Prison for stealing a tractor from a construction site in Chula Vista. And, right now, you're headed for Madera.

The door to Room Six swings open silently. It's unlocked. Dennis and Warren don't give a shit. They're sitting cross-legged on the bed, two grown men in their boxers, sweating, shuddering, smoking meth. Normally, they look like computer programmers from Akron. Windbreakers and Hawaiian shirts. Wire-rimmed glasses. Socks in Birkenstocks. Dennis is only thirty-eight, but his shoulder-length hair is dark gray streaked with white. He keeps it pushed behind his ears. Warren likes to wear sun visors. He knows card tricks.

The bowl of the lightbulb pipe is black where Warren's lighter flame licks it. Warren grins at a square burn on his thumb from the lighter. The facial tic at the corner of his mouth is back and makes his grin look insane. Warren's cockeyed. Cockeyed-stoned. He exhales a puff of used smoke and hands the pipe to Dennis. Neither of them speaks. You don't hear a sound but the lighter, the pipe hiss, and the tick of the air conditioner in the wall. Chemical meth-smell hangs in the air. Dennis exhales and stands on the bed. He turns on the TV and starts jumping, flipping channels with the remote. This makes Warren fall over backwards. He gasps and curses but doesn't get up. Instead, he stretches out on the floor between the bed and the wall. You hear the hiss of the pipe.

The bathroom is cool and dark. Thankfully, it has a tub. You take your jacket and shirt off. You're careful to remove your wallet, keys, and the thin survival knife you found in the truck's glove box. This won't be the first time you've used your clothing as a mattress in a strange bathtub. You curl up on your side and pull the shower curtain closed. Outside, Dennis yells at the television. Warren yells at Dennis. They will do this for five, six hours, then crash.

It's a long way to freedom with a girlfriend and son behind you and Madera in the front. You might be an accessory to murder. Accessory. The word tumbles around in your head. You hear it the way one hears a foreign term and can't forget it. The word for prison in German is *Gefängnis*. You took German in high school from Mr. Antonucci. *Du mußt nicht ins Gefängnis gehen*, he'd say and laugh. Don't go to prison. *Gefängnis*, you think, accessory.

"Szechwan chicken is not fucking fried!" screams Dennis.

"Fuck that. The fucking chef knows what he's doing," screams Warren. "He's the *chef*, man."

It's been almost six hours with sleep as a distant fantasy and the two assholes in the next room arguing about (1) the *Musical Chef*; (2) the differences between Fiats and Škodas; and (3) whether Nixon was better than our current chief executive—*Fucking-A he wasn't. Nixon was an idiot—Fuck you, Dennis, Bush is a FAGGOT*—with the occasional *Learn your shit!* and *Why don't you just shut the fuck up?* thrown in. Yes, you frown, pulling your knees up closer to your chin, yes, why don't you?

Then, finally, when silence comes, it's total, sudden, and ominous. You dress, put your things back in your pockets, and creep out of the bathroom, cheering yourself with images of Dennis and Warren contorted in a final death-embrace, hands around each other's throats, neck veins still bulged out. Instead, it's the usual scene. Dennis is spread-eagled on the bed, head hanging upside down off the edge, snuffling with his mouth open. Warren's on his side, sleeping on the round table under the window. He didn't bother to brush away the wrappers from the vending machine food and looks like he's been sleeping at the bottom of a trash can. You walk out of the room, shut the door, and stare at the low-slung peel of moon just above the horizon. Maybe you should call Chris again. You're out of change. You'd have to call collect.

The woman in the motel office is also stoned. How many times have you seen this in the late-night offices of motels, trailer parks, campgrounds? The bored, slightly pathetic life-form behind the desk, hooked into bad TV and whatever happens to be on the smoking menu that evening. There's usually nobody around, and it's a real bummer when somebody steps in with some problem. She's thought ahead, has a cigarette burning in the ashtray to cover up the hash smell. But hash is hash, as a wise man once said. In your humble opinion, hash is a good thing. Let there be hash.

She looks over at you, wishing the one thing in the world you won't do is speak. You mosey over to the urn of free coffee and get a cup. The coffee tastes like hot, bitter plastic, but it warms you from the inside, which is always the best way to get warm. When you were a kid, warm felt like that. Your dad would make instant coffee on the kitchen counter in the morning—thin and steaming, without sugar. Was it his way of saying, *I'm sorry your worthless mother OD'd in your bed and you had to come home from school and find her there?* Was it his way of saying, *I apologize for the stints in various orphanages while I did six months in prison here, a year there?* Maybe he wasn't trying to say anything but *Drink up.* You've thought about these things for years. You can take all the time you need, think about it for the rest of your life if you want. It might take that long to figure out your childhood. The important thing is, standing in the office of the Apache Motel, looking at the sad array of yellowed tourist brochures from fifteen years ago, you feel warm. You've got coffee. You've got a son named Jessup. You're not in jail. You're not dead.

"I suppose there's something you want."

"Nothing," you say. "Coffee." You hold up the Styrofoam cup and smile on your way out. She turns back to her show without a word. Her cigarette has burned down to the filter, leaving a two-inch worm of ash. Doesn't look like she smoked any of it. She's in her thirties, getting curves where she shouldn't, platinum-dyed hair tied back in a band.

Outside, you look at her through the windowpanes

in the door. She's sitting there, not blinking, staring at the television as if she's part of it. A machine could do her job. Someday, you think, a machine will. You notice a blue push-button with a black circular base beside the door. Around it, *Press Button if Offise Closed* is written in Magic Marker. You walk down the side of the motel, following the wires running from the button. The wires are covered in the same tan paint as the rest of the motel.

Ah. You feel good for the first time since you started this trip. If Dennis were here, you might even consider discussing whether you're about to enter a quantum state. Or, rather, whether the blonde's cottage is, because that's where the bell wires end, and you've still got that survival knife in your pocket. While she sits over in the motel office, the rest of the cosmos waits in one of Dennis' probabilistic equations—with and without her hearing, you snap the latch on the cottage's screen door and pry the survival knife into the lock; with and without her getting up to check (probably *not*—if you want to talk about likely hits from a very probable hash pipe); with and consequently without some interesting items, which she should have made a lot more secure.

You smile, picturing how irritated Dennis would be with you narrating all the possible outcomes of the situation as you easily, absently, twist the knife in the ancient lock and shoulder the door open. *Probabilistically speaking*, you'd say to Dennis, dogs simultaneously wagging and not wagging their tails misses the point. You pause in the darkness of the living room and think about Dennis' hypothetical. Who cares what's behind Door Number One? That's the real question. Nerve gas? A yipping dachshund? If you want to know, twist a knife in the lock. If you don't, let poisoned, radioactive dachshunds lie.

It's a small cottage, but the living room seems large in the dark. A digital clock face glows red from a bookshelf. You hear a slow drip-plop from the kitchen, and decide to feel your way to the bedroom first. What's wrong with a little thievery, really, everything being equal and equally thieved? Money. Time. The Beatles thieving Little Richard. The US thieving Mexico thieving the Indians, body and soul.

Everybody thieving oil and oil thieving right back. Children thieve the future from their parents as parents thieve the past. Dracula pulls up in front of the blood bank, and the President invades Iraq. It's the way you live, the way we live, the way we're all going to die—thieving one more taste of life in this desert of trouble and mistakes until death gets its own hustle on. The only downside is getting caught reminding people of the truth, not just *your* truth but everybody's: the world is a criminal. If your son were here, you'd sit him down and tell him just that. The whole world, Jessup. The very earth.

The bedroom smells like cigarettes and strong perfume, and it cheers you right away. Your new best friend has cases on her pillows. Good. You strip both pillows in the dark. Now you have two sacks. Tossing a house, really stripping it, might take an hour or two. But if you don't want the gold out of someone's teeth (and normally you don't—too burdensome, too hard to get rid of every last, little thing), it ought to take ten minutes, less. Appliances. Jewelry. Grandpa's roll of bills under the mattress. People have no imagination. They're sheep. They buy the fake Ajax can to hold their pension and go to sleep feeling like it's safer than the bank.

Sheep. Like this girl—diamond earrings, five hundred, and a dime bag rolled into an old sock in her panty drawer— the place you usually look after the mattress. Someone should tell her she's right. The bank isn't safe. No place is. Someone should tell her, if she put down the hash pipe, just for tonight, and did her rounds, you wouldn't be able to rob her blind, and there's no FDIC on an Ajax can.

"Baa," you say to the living room, bagging the DVD player and some nice stereo components—far too nice for a motel manager, which proves your point yet again. Who really owns anything? You're a goddamn social revolutionary, quantum dog state or not. You pull the clock's power cord out of the wall, wrap it around the clock, and put the clock in your sack. The entire escapade has taken about twelve minutes in the dark.

On your way out, you turn on the bathroom sink and the shower. This is great—a little, original twist. Most people will run straight into the bathroom and stare dumbly at the floor, going, "Baa." Did the pipes explode? Did the toilet overflow? (Oh shit!) Meanwhile, you're several miles down the road, feeling good for having played your role in the great, daily sacrament of human crime.

Back in the office, she's still sitting behind the desk, slack-jawed, watching television. You look at her again through the glass in the door, then enter, leaving your sacks leaning against the wall outside.

"What's on?" Another cup of coffee seems good. It *swooshes* into the cup.

"*Real Life*. It's a reality show." She doesn't look at you. Her words sound stilted, deliberately linked, as if she thought about each one before adding it to the sentence. You wonder if she might be thinking about just how much attention it's going to take for you to leave smoothly, without a fuss, without screwing up her high.

"Reality, eh?" You've heard of this kind of show, but you've never seen one of them. You haven't watched TV in about ten years. "Does that mean other shows aren't real?"

"Of course they're not real. Where've you been?"

"I work nights."

She turns and gives you a long, slow stare, one part disbelief, two parts weariness.

"If we can talk about them, aren't they real?"

"What the fuck do you mean?" Hostile. She swivels all the way around to face you. You are a problem. Now she has to deal with you.

You take a sip of coffee and smile, stepping back. "Shows are real shows, right?"

"Are you looking for something? 'Cause I don't have anything for you. Understand what I'm saying?"

"Just talking." You shrug. Smile. Move toward the door.

She stands up, brow knitted, concentrating. "Look," she says to the desk, "shows are shows. Some shows are real. Some are all made up. Is that what you're asking?"

"So what's real life, then?"

"They just take a camera into some place, like a store, and let it sit."

You put your hand on the doorknob. *"That's* crazy. What do you see?"

She is convinced you're an idiot. She gestures with the backs of her hands, fingers up, as if to show how evident it all is. She looks like a surgeon about to operate. "Everything. They went to this butcher shop. People came in and said fucked-up things to the butchers. Then they cut some meat."

"Like nasty things?"

"This one chick goes, 'I want a piece of rump,' and the butcher, all covered in blood and shit, goes, 'Me, too.' How fucked up is that?" She's still standing as if she's about to pull a can of mace out from behind the desk, but the corner of her mouth curls in glassy amusement. Thinking about it makes her laugh and cough.

"Ever want them to come here?"

"And film what? Me watching the show? That would mess with your head."

"It sure would." You toast her with the Styrofoam cup and walk out, picking up your sacks on the way to the room.

Baa.

The truth happens. Sometimes, absolute truth happens. And, when it does, you've decided you don't want to be anywhere close. Fifty megatons of truth with a half-life of regret for eternity. When the truth comes down, it drops like a bomb or a burning flare. Facts that follow you. Fallout in perpetuity, in the midnight hour, staring at a dark ceiling or out the window of a stolen truck, thinking of all the people you've robbed, defrauded, screwed. Of how you went to college for two years and could have wound up better.

Sitting in the passenger's seat of the jacked semi as Dennis drives it up the 99, you look out at tractor dealerships, broken motels, heavy machinery yards in the orange-white envelope of a burning San Joaquin Valley afternoon. You think of the original driver, pale in his own headlights, as if sculpted in wax. You imagine his upturned face burning white at the bottom of the ditch where you threw him, the ditch itself like a ghost town. Marking the spot: *this is where they left me to die,* the truth finally come down. Burning where it fell. Clinging to the earth for as long as it could. Not your truth. Not anyone's. But *the* truth. Absolute truth this time—hideous, brutal, and rare.

Regret for eternity. How much for taking that poor chick's DVD player and pot and clocks? More, you're sure, for having drawn her just the smallest bit out of her bolt hole of hash and *Real Life*. Eternity plus five.

"So I've been thinking," says Dennis, "about the possibilities. You know. With the dog."

"You're still on this?"

"On what? What the hell, man? Don't you care about the meaning of *life*?"

"That sounds like a show."

"Work with me. We've got a dead-or-not-dead dog trying to wag his tail. We need to solve this shit." Dennis downshifts and grins. The silver cap on his right incisor is turning black. His eyes are still bloodshot from the meth.

Warren's stolen brown Datsun two cars behind is holding steady in the side mirror. It looks like it's been smoking meth, too. And Warren inside it: hair straight up, face partly swollen as if he's been punched a few times which, in a way, he has. Warren got up this morning like *Night of the Living Dead*. Dennis laughed, said, "Rise! Rise!" To which, Warren responded with his usual, "Fuck. You."

Plus five. Plus five with fire and perdition. With your whole ancestral line for generations back, through dispossessed French Huguenots and amoral Scotsmen—the balance of whom were probably hung as thieves or burned as liars. And drawn. And quartered. And blamed. And mortared. And taken off all books of contributing members before being dismembered. But not before they could breed the next generation into this confusion. The confused, jagged screech of a newborn slapped hard on the ass so it takes its first breath—what better way to symbolize life than this? *That hurt. I don't feel good. And this place very clearly sucks.*

You're thinking about all this, letting it tumble through your brain, while Jimbo checks the truck. A slight man, Jimbo, slight and low-talking. He mumbles. He murmurs. He stands by the truck and says things to Andre, who nods like he's taking dictation. Maybe Andre is. There's no telling what a relationship could be between a beady-eyed, marsupial-faced thug and a little man from Nigeria with colored braids and a dark green polo. All that matters is Jimbo has the cash. That's all you need to know. And Jimbo's got a kid named Omar who's fidgeting with the latch on the truck, overexcited, asking you too many questions: "Hey, man, you do this a lot? It looks like the money's good." Omar has no purpose, you think. Omar should not exist.

Andre goes to get the payment while Jimbo and Warren talk off to the side, Jimbo's voice like the hum of distant equipment, Warren gesturing with his hands.

"It's fine," you say and look at the kid.

Omar nods, uses his palm to wipe the sweat off the top of his head. Dennis yawns and lights a cigarette. The warehouse is empty except for the truck. And it's big—as big as a hangar. Might have been a factory once or a machine shop for heavy equipment. You watch Andre get smaller as he walks across the cement floor, way back to the other side of the warehouse, where the dark office door stands open. Then he lumbers back, carrying the bag. The wrinkled paper grocery bag. The bag of bags.

The bag with the money.

Everybody gets paid, and everybody gets happy. Andre buys both sacks from you for a crisp hundred dollar bill off his roll before he gets in the truck with Jimbo. You watch them go, Kenworth ghost town vanishing to the underworld. The warehouse is dead silent. It's all over, done, and no problems. You tell yourself you should feel good.

You get into the passenger seat of Warren's Datsun. Warren slides behind the wheel and tries to get the engine to turn over, Dennis and Omar in back. Omar's nervous, trying to act like he's cool. But he's wired, staring at the three of you when he thinks you're not looking.

"I gotta ditch this shit in Bakersfield. I'll drop anybody on the way." Warren sighs, stretches. Nobody says a word or counts any money. You look at Dennis' eyes in the rearview mirror as the car pulls out and leaves a cloud of white smoke behind it that reminds you of meth. Dennis is getting freaked out by Omar. You're mildly surprised Dennis waits until you get on the 99 before he starts messing with the kid.

"Why you lookin' at me?" he says to Omar in a half-whisper. "Don't you fucking look at me."

"Sorry." Omar looks like he might piss himself.

"Why you here, anyway?" Dennis pulls the .45 and presses Omar's face against the window with it. "Why the *fuck* are you here? Why didn't you leave with Andre?"

The kid doesn't say anything. He clamps his jaw shut. You turn around in your seat and watch. Omar's got a sweat stain around the neck of his T-shirt and straight down the front like a ruff.

"That's a good question," says Warren, driving with his left elbow on the door and his face propped in his hand. He sounds like he's about to fall asleep, still hungover from all the happy meth.

"Pull over," says Dennis. "I think I'm gonna shoot this asshole right here."

"No," says Omar, squeezing his eyes shut.

"Okay," sighs Warren. The Datsun rolls to a stop in another cloud of smoke.

How many times, you wonder, has something like this happened on the 99 South?

"Get the fuck out," screams Dennis as he runs around the back of the car, gun in hand.

Omar tries to lock the door, but Dennis yanks it open and pulls him out by his foot.

Omar's crying, on his knees, with Dennis pushing the .45 into his forehead in broad daylight.

"You pathetic piece of shit," screams Dennis over air and traffic, "gimme your wallet." A semi, not unlike the one you've been driving for the past several days, makes the Datsun rock like a boat. Dennis whacks Omar in the side of the head with the gun to snap him out of his crying. A passing car leans on its horn. You imagine the call: *Police! Send the SWAT team! There's a guy getting executed on the 99!*

"Come on. This is taking forever." You yell it into the wind, not wanting to get out and make yourself more identifiable, hoping Dennis doesn't actually shoot him. But, by the time you say it, Dennis is already in the backseat. Warren hits the gas and whips into the slow lane. Behind you, Omar is still kneeling but bent over, forehead on his hands as if in prayer.

"Look at that." Dennis has Omar's watch on. This is the real Dennis, you think—not the philosophical guy who likes to take it easy and talk about dogs wagging their tails. This is the criminal. You wonder where you fall on Dennis' scale and whether you'd have left Omar bent over and weeping in the heat.

"That's not a real Rolex," you say. "A real Rolex doesn't have its hands click forward like that. They're smooth."

"So? Shit, I knew that."

Warren and Dennis start laughing. You laugh, too, because not laughing when a crazy meth-addicted asshole is sitting behind you with a loaded gun is not an option. You tell yourself this might be it. No more truckjacking. Fuck the money. A box of high-end Louis Vuittons doesn't shoot you in the head.

Dennis is still laughing when he taps you on the shoulder with the butt of the .45.

"Wasn't loaded," he says and shows you the empty space where the clip should be. He makes a hard face. "You like my gangsta-gangsta?"

"Yeah, man." You smile: funny joke. "I believed it."

"I've got talent." He takes his wire-rimmed glasses out of his leather case and polishes them with his shirt.

You nod and keep smiling.

These trips have made you close to $50,000. But none of them were as violent as this one. You think of Omar bent over on the side of the highway. You should put him out of your mind. You tell yourself you've been Omar. You tell yourself that if Omar keeps his mouth shut and learns a thing or two, he might just live to be you.

The Man in Africa

I bought Lotto tickets. I read sad poems and cursed.

Later, I'd tell people that this was all during my Blue Period, where everything eventually came back to porn, where German leisure pants with gigantic blue trapezoids started to seem okay in the privacy of my own home. Blue because I wanted love and money but got a blue plastic boat cover for Christmas from my grandfather in Baden Baden along with the pants. Blue for all the things I kept trying to say without saying to ex-fiancée Lori's answering machine in the blue hours of the night. Blue for all the yeahs and I-told-you-sos of the world served back to me by sarcastic waiters in blue aprons. Blue because I didn't own a boat to put under the boat cover. And blue because that's exactly how things went. You wanted gold. You wanted suffrage and diversity and the warm sun and chocolates for everyone; instead you got a blue nightmare, everybody's face closed and creased like good-bye stationery with blue trim from an ex-fiancée, living now in Point Azul, where the ocean reflects the sky.

Every day, I hoped life would improve, and every day it didn't. My neighbor, Sid, an ex-long-haul trucker who'd had a nervous breakdown and found God, came over in the evenings with a case of Olympia because he didn't own a TV. Changing his life for Jesus meant giving up his sinful trucking ways in favor of becoming a cobbler or a farmer—something biblical and profound—only he didn't like touching other people's old shoes and he was offended by manure. So he set out to become a tailor. Now he was more of a seamstress, his electric Singer whirring and clicking at all hours on the other side of the wall.

Sid belched a Sid-belch, a low, wet one, and didn't apologize. But I wasn't asking. He didn't tell me about salvation, and I didn't mention his constant belching and farting. We drank Olympia, watched CNN. Half the time, I didn't even know he was there, caught up as I was in the difficulties of my blue life and my overall failure at everything.

I suppose I tolerated his visits because everyone I knew thought I was worthless in some way, and I generally agreed with them. The sum of Sid's criticism, however, was: "Will, you know, you should get that shirt altered. It takes less than two minutes to put on one button. I hate for you to hear it like this, but it'll make that shirt look a whole lot better." And then nothing for the rest of the night. I could live with that.

Tonight, CNN had been interviewing troops back from the Persian Gulf, who'd begun to have visions, possibly due to the use of so much depleted uranium in the rounds.

"It's basically, uh, we feel, having been there on the ground, a lot of us have come to feel, basically, seriously, that God is a dirty bomb." twenty-two-year-old Sgt. Evan Fulton. Hair in tufts. Sunken eyes.

"Excuse me, did I just hear you say that God is a dirty bomb?"

"Uh, yeah, basically."

Sid moaned. "Oh man. This is it." Olympia can poised in front of his lips. "The end times."

"Hey," I flicked the channel up one to *Cops*. "You better take it easy with that fire and brimstone shit."

Something had to be done.

I took a singles cruise to Catalina, telling myself it was the thing. But it wasn't the thing, and I wound up drunk in the corner, yelling over the music with a balding French woman who didn't believe the moon landing had happened.

"Accept it," she said. "It was all just simulation."

"Stimulation?" I asked.

"You're all the same," she said.

I drove up the coast with a children's theater troupe, playing Boy Jim in *The Pirates of O'Claire*. No one complained that I was long past boyhood and that the culottes I wore made me look like an aged clown from a failing backwoods circus—until a kid in the audience squeaked out "He's no boy!" when I crept from my barrel in scene two. For the rest of the afternoon, waves of eight-year-old laughter came in all the wrong places.

I signed up for Buddhist golf lessons and got to the point of realizing that the desire to hit a birdie was my main obstacle in achieving detachment. When I'd put one squarely in the lake, my caddy would wrap his orange robes more tightly around himself, clasp his hands, and smile beatifically: "Do you not see that it is not the ball that traverses the distance, rather, it is only yourself?" After three days of that, I nodded and threw the club in after it.

In theory, I still had a job teaching prescriptive grammar at Mesa Del Mar, a high school in the suburbs of San Diego. It was a good job until I browbeat the strong safety of the football team to tears and had to settle with his parents in arbitration. I took a forced leave of absence. They took him to Provençe. And I'd have to take a psych evaluation before coming back next semester.

Sam Perganov, the principal, had been all too clear: "Don't think of it as a suspension, Will. Think of it as a chance to get back in touch with your inner imperatives." Sam: who benched 350 and could never go back to Odessa. "You've got to learn how to relax, mellow out a bit, work with the students instead of viewing them with such hostility." He cracked his knuckles and I nodded politely.

What kind of high school suspends its teachers for speaking harshly to a student? I asked this over and over, but I knew the answer. People were getting nervous. People were out of touch with their inner imperatives. The kids might have already gained access to caseless ammo and Belgian anti-tank weapons—not hard to come by, I hear, on the playground. There were rumors that a band of sophomores was circulating a bootlegged copy of *The Battle of Algiers*, that they had their own handshake, that they'd dug a network of catacombs under the faculty lot. They said the kids could even recognize the local candidates for mayor and knew what voting was.

Something had to be done. The PTA had to unite, stay the course, communicate in ways that everybody could easily understand, reestablish decency and homespun American values everywhere. To this end, Mesa Del Mar did away with art, band, and English classes, replacing them with community service, music appreciation, and prescriptive grammar. Speech was limited to delivering pre-nineteenth century Celtic valedictions. The school went on permanent orange alert. There was talk of metal detectors, random body searches, loyalty oaths, a guard tower on the upper field. German Shepherds.

Maybe because of all the strife and upheaval, at various low moments, in little outtakes of despair, I worried that I'd never get in touch with my inner self, that the enlightenment Sam Perganov said I needed was forever beyond me. I worried that when it got down to taking whatever come-back-to-work polygraph they no doubt planned to give me under a scorching interrogation lamp in the faculty lounge, they'd write my name on the floor in red chalk and I'd be so nervous I'd stutter, answer all the questions wrong, and FAIL, FAIL, FAIL, FAIL, FAIL.

It got humid. Then it rained for a week.

Fifteen days had passed in my mandatory leave of absence. And I'd begun getting up at ten in the morning, spending all day in my pajamas surfing the internet. Since I was not, technically, jobless, I felt I should be looking up new ways of presenting The Common Grammatical Errors, novel ways to split an infinitive, unique applications for the em dash. But all I found was porn.

Always and forever there are the great golden felicitations of internet porn to revive you. One click and you're whisked away to a shimmering paradise where nothing is forbidden, where interactive webcams offer you orgasmic surveillance and total control: live college dorm girls in bondage, four girls and two guys, three guys and one girl, three guys who look like girls, naked people in Hungarian leather who send you instant messages, naked people in bulky black shoes who want to know: *Are you cut? Uncut?*, defecation, exfoliation, weightlifters, anorexics, amateurs, analinguists, anal linguists, downloading and uploading, The Pleasures of the Orient, Fully Interactive Orgies with Indigenous Peoples. You control the cameras. You control the action, sahib.

With the interactive sites, you could change the angle of the shots, instant message the participants with suggestions, and they might stop to answer:

> Turbodog: Cindie, I think you should be on your
> back.
> Cindie Foxx: Oh, yes, Turbodog, that's a *good* idea.

Of course, there's no accounting for taste. Whenever I logged off, I had to face up to the brutal reality of being in my pajamas at 2:30 PM. For the first time in my life, I was on forced leave, forced to relax, and I could give the information superhighway my undivided attention. I started a blog. I called ex-fiancée Lori and asked her answering machine for its opinion. I thought seriously about air quality and emission standards all over the world. I walked around my apartment and looked at discolored creases in the walls. Nothing is worse than a vacation.

I kept my TV on CNN, volume way down. The glassy-eyed talking heads with wrinkled mouths comforted me like distant aunts and uncles at a wake who don't know what to say, their voices just low enough to make no sense. Mmmffuga . . . mmmimosa . . . have a sherdgu . . . mekkeh . . . last time in grasm . . . hbongoggrd . . . rrrmurdel . . . ah, exactly, brnl . . . Mimosa?

Couldn't be. On screen they were showing recent footage of Japanese protesters being gassed, flame-blossom Molotov cocktails in the street, sci-fi riot cops behind tower shields. I pictured Wolf Blitzer saying, "Why don't we all just go down and get a mimosa? The girls from the BBC are already there, dog. And they *party*." Two-for-one Molotov cocktails. Happy hour in Aomori Prefecture.

On the other TV (the backup set: be prepared), the local San Diego news seemed just as grim but in a maudlin way. Concerned parents and faculty were holding a candlelit prayer-in in Mesa Del Mar's gym, singing "We Shall Overcome." Their reasons for doing this were unclear to me. Maybe it was due to the group of dissident sophomores and their tunnels. Maybe it was something else entirely. Everyone had fat green ribbons tied around their left wrists. The real question was, why wasn't I invited? I'm cool. I could go to a prayer-in.

> Turbodog: Cindie, would you go to a prayer-in with
>   me?
> Cindie Foxx: I love prayer-ins, Turbodog.

It's an indisputable fact of life that we all need to be watched. Webcams, surveillance, the sense that somebody has an eye on us is a good thing. It helps us flag the warning signs. It helps protect us from ourselves. That's why, when Susan Thorrson called me and said "What's that clicking on the line? Do you hear that clicking?" I checked my Caller ID, saw "IDENTIFICATION BLOCKED," and knew immediately it was her. I also knew that the clicking didn't matter. In the new openness of a perfectly surveilled culture, everything, even sexual fetishes, will be style points—like gourmet beers or a choice of socks: *are you really going for the argyle today? You're so naughty.*

And why else would Susan be calling me? Actually, she, too, was a teacher of prescriptive grammar at Mesa Del Mar, so she could have been calling for any prescriptive reason. But, since I was looking at *Amateur Hardcore Webcams* right then, I just assumed . . . and the assumption was natural and okay and nothing to be ashamed of.

"Don't mind the clicking," I said. "Susan, I sense the reason for your call. I took these Buddhist golf lessons and, I don't know, they gave me a kind of intuition."

"This isn't Susan. I don't know any Susan." She hung up.

Two minutes later, she called back. "This is not Susan," she said. "Understand?"

I said I understood completely. I said I understood more than she knew and that it was okay and that I felt I was finally coming to know her inner imperatives.

The webcams pulsed in the darkness of my bedroom. Cindie Foxx was gone and now Pretty Pouty Petra was doing a striptease wrapped in the Confederate flag. Someone off-camera lobbed dried apricots at her breasts, breasts that looked far older than the rest of her—even though the site assured me that "All Models are 18-20 Years of Age." Every now and then, she'd stagger and take a swig off the Heineken she kept around the corner of the white sofa behind her. Amateur webcams. Amateurs, not professionals, are allowed to drink Heineken when stripping off the Confederate flag. It was fascinating.

"We need to talk," said Susan. "A lot of rumors are going around."

"Of course. We should talk. We are, after all, consenting adults."

"I think I'm in trouble," she said. "Certain issues have come to light."

"Nonsense. There's no reason to feel ashamed about anything. Meet me for dinner tonight, and we'll embrace this new openness together. I've been wanting to embrace it with you, for some time."

Petra was now on the sofa, straddling a muscle-bound military man with a bristling crewcut while she twirled the Confederate flag over her head like a lasso and guffawed.

Susan said she'd be by around eight, but she sounded disoriented, maybe ecstatic. Maybe she was finally coming to realize that her true inner imperatives had little, if anything, to do with prescription and everything to do with visualization, fantasization, tantalization.

"I think I'm being watched."

"That's okay." I said, "A lot of people are into that."

In order to keep up with the new security improvements, I'd bought a Land Rover with the last of my savings. It wasn't quite bulletproof, not quite a Hummer, but it still had enough solidity to discourage sniper fire. I threw a good tint job on it the day I drove it off the lot. You'd have to aim straight through the front windshield if you wanted to target my head.

I parked the Rover across from Mesa Del Mar, cracked the side window just enough for my binoculars, and checked things out. They'd fired the old crossing guard, substituting a senior on top of the administration building with his own binoculars and a notebook. Every time I did this, I watched him watching me. He was always there, recording anything suspicious. I imagined him taking down my license plate, my description, noting the time. I stuck my hand out and waved. He took that down, too.

On my visits I often noticed unmarked vehicles with zoom lenses pointing out their windows at the principal's office, the nurse's office, the upper field. Snap, snap, snap: oh yes, we have pictures. *Fotographia*. We have your sons and daughters. We better than have them. They've been uploaded, data-mined, ported, resolved, pattern recognized, plotted-and-slotted, trajectorized. We know about the sophomore tunnels. We have animatronicized the secret handshake. We're watching your little Che right now via our supersexy Hungarian_leather.ru uplink.

Tension was thick in the air. People covered their faces, looked down, spent as little time in the open as possible. Everywhere on campus blinds were swaying, drapes had telling spaces, figures disappeared behind corners. But I wanted to get up and dance. I wanted to get out of my high-end, high-target-profile sport utility vehicle and do a tarantella along the tops of cars parked parallel to the administration building while people off screen lobbed dried apricots at me. Dance like some pixelated Charlie Chaplin. You control the action, sahib.

I got out of the Land Rover and stood on the sidewalk, looking up at my friend on the roof across the street. Part of me knew this was suicidal. One does not stand on a sidewalk beside an open SUV door in Southern California and not expect to be a target: bad positioning, leaving oneself vulnerable to rabid dogs and carjackings, government snipers, tsetse flies, chronic masturbators in second-floor windows. But something about my young accomplice with the field glasses and notebook moved me. He was a tragic yet hopeful figure, scribbling feverishly, trying to get it all down, as if that were possible.

I raised my hand in peace, noting Sam Perganov's stricken white face peeking around his office blinds. And I wondered if Sam was joyous or terrified or joyously terrified like me, about to burst, as my feet did a little shuffle on the pavement. I wished I could step into his skin to see me seeing him seeing me. I grinned and waved at both Sam and my buddy on the roof. I wished Pretty Pouty Petra were there, all wrapped up in stars 'n bars and full of Heinekens.

Turbodog: Cindie?

Cindie Foxx: Yes, Turbodog?

Turbodog: Do you think Paul Virilio was right when he wrote that systems of modern surveillance have precipitated a new obliviousness to the element of interpretative subjectivity that is always at play in the act of looking?

Cindie Foxx: Oh, yes, Turbodog, that's a good idea.

And here was Susan Thorrson sitting across the table from me, Cantonese food imminent. And I knew that one *cannot* have flirtatious *tête-à-tête* with svelte female grammarian while obsessing about surveillance. So I tried to put it out of my mind, but I was feeling a little shaky, a little less than fine.

Susan seemed about to cry. It was fairly clear that there would be no naked self-realizations after dinner at my apartment, no Heinekens, no uninhibited exchanges on a white sofa while we photographed each other and guffawed. Consequently, I felt like I should either be recording our conversation for my own protection or escaping through the kitchen. I was sure I had done nothing wrong.

Susan looked both beautiful and disturbed in the red vinyl booth, sitting up against the gigantic Cantonese lobster tank. She sighed and stared at her plate of orange chicken and shrimp fried rice. She seemed so unhappy I didn't have the heart to tell her the truth about orange chicken, about how each cubic centimeter of it would soon be fulminating in her pores. Zinc oxide, copper gluconate, monosodium glutamate, manganese sulfate, pyriodoxide hydrochloride, yellow-6, blue-12, all smoking its way through her system like Chinese mustard gas. Carcinogenic. Morbid degeneration. Kills one in six albino test mice. She raised a dainty, well-measured bite of chicken to a perfect Pouty Petra mouth.

"Are you listening to me? They've got me on tape," she said.

I watched her chew, heard the hissing of woks in the kitchen. They were cooking with napalm, whole sections of jungle going up in towers of fire just so *jefe* could get his tangy chicken. And in the meantime Susan's cell walls collapsed, vacuoles filling with boiling blue-12 death fluid.

"You shouldn't get upset," I said. "Turn yourself in for whatever you've done and you'll feel better."

"As of this morning, I *know* they're listening to me." For a moment, she looked less pretty and pouty and more like ex-fiancée Lori: eyes narrowed, calculating, figuring her options.

Susan lowered her voice and leaned in: "I used the phrase 'subject-predicate' but, on their equipment, I don't know. Every time I used it, it sounded like 'subject-proletariat.' They played the tape for me, my own voice. They think I'm in with that student group. I said I didn't know a damn thing about any tunnels."

She swallowed shrimp fried rice. I watched her throat as she did it: napalm over the rainforest. Albino test mice buried in unmarked graves.

"Level with them first thing tomorrow," I said. "Just tell the truth and remember, they have the technology. They're *always* watching. It's for our own protection. It's important that you understand that." Enunciating over the saltshaker, I thought of Sam Perganov sitting in the back of an unmarked van smiling and nodding.

"They want me to take a lie detector test. They've got an old reel-to-reel in a closet in the gym. The whole place is wired. How do you think they got me on tape?"

Was the black lobster crawling right up to the aquarium

glass over her shoulder so it could get a better look at me? The Cantonese music sounded sped up.

"Is there something wrong with you? You haven't eaten a thing."

"That lobster," I said, "doesn't have a name. One of these days, somebody's going to take it out and knock its head open or boil it alive. But, for now, we can see it and it can see us. Everybody's safe. We know where we stand. Right?" A trickle of sweat ran down the back of my neck.

She glanced over her shoulder at the lobster, then started inching out of the booth, a frozen smile on her face.

Later, I would tell people that Susan Thorrson and I met for some innocent Cantonese chicken. I'd say I had nothing to do with the lobster and, while its death was tragic, I have no knowledge of any prior communications with it or its associates. Cameras in my face. Toxic air. My name on the ground in red chalk.

"How's the orange chicken?" I asked.

I walked straight home from my dinner with Susan thinking that maybe, just maybe, the truth about orange chicken was at the very heart of the matter. Too much manganese sulfate and your brow begins to slope, cheeks elongate, ears grow large. Too much copper gluconate and you can't stop talking, too little and you start to float. Exceed the recipe for pyriodoxide hydrochloride and you're a yipping dachshund, while a massive overdose of zinc oxide gives fluency in Middle English and impedes higher brain functions. *Thow thynkest now, how sholde I don al this?* But the ugly truth: the subject-proletariat has no idea what's in their chicken or who's dipping their woks in smoldering vats of napalm by the light of the moon.

Running fingers through my hair, I questioned everything, wondering if these were actually my thoughts and emotions or just additives, blue-12, yellow-6 bubbling across the brainpan. Was this a test? Even now, was I being recorded? Was all of this going down in some permanent record—"Will Dent's Reactions to Various Psycho-Chemical Stimuli"—along with my handwriting homework from second grade and how many moving violations I had as a teenager? Later, if I tried to describe these feelings, would people understand me? Would they even hear the words? Or would my mouth be moving to a different language, dubbed like in the kung fu movies of my youth? I'd be screaming:

Help me, I fear this is a hostile world!

Help me, I fear anything might explode at any minute! That there are mics in the palm trees! That Sam Perganov knows which side of the bed I like to sleep on! But they'd hear: *Damn you! Come out and fight! You think you know kung fu?!*

I opened my door and the place was ransacked. All the drawers in my scuffed porter's desk were upside-down on the floor, curtains ripped, refrigerator on its side and hissing. I wondered what the ransackers could possibly have been looking for when they pulled up the floorboards, and what sort of tool could have made such splintered edges. How long had it taken them to decide to slash the sofa cushions? Was this before or after they cut open the mattress? And why had they gone through the trouble of clogging the toilet with wadded-up newspaper and flushing it repeatedly until it overflowed? Of course, there were no answers. The refrigerator could only hiss.

Staring at the holes in the floor, I dialed ex-fiancée Lori but, of course, her machine answered for her. I dialed Susan. "If you're listening to me, don't call back." I'd begun to preface all my calls with this. If she didn't call me back, I'd already requested it. If she did, she was already at a disadvantage. Ingenious, I know. "I don't understand why they've ransacked my apartment. I've done nothing wrong. You know how well-groomed I am, how much love I have for teaching prescriptive grammar and for . . . the principal."

As I stared at the wreckage, I tried to picture who could have done such a thing and realized I hadn't checked all the rooms. My leg started jiggling. I began to sweat all over again.

"I think of our school as more than just a high school.

It's a growing experience for young adults. And our principal, he's like a father, a real leader."

That black lobster looking at me through the glass. One of these days, they're going to take it out back and knock its head open, boil it alive.

"I didn't mean to browbeat anyone on the *football* team. I go to all the games. I love my students. Those kids are my life."

In fact, I would have liked to get the strong safety on tape. Maybe start a webcam: www.amateurbrowbeatings. com. Interrogation lamp, name chalked at his feet: *You! Don't you know what an obscure pronoun reference is?! Did you have any idea what you were doing when you let that participle dangle? The violence? The depravity? Did it occur to you that you were completely destroying that sentence? Are you not ashamed? Horrified at your behavior? . . . We have been watching you for some time.*

I hung up gently, as gently as I could with sweaty palms, nerves clenching the pit of my stomach, trying to recall the last time I ate or what, if anything, I'd had to drink beyond a sip of lukewarm souchong with Susan and the lobster. In the bathroom, I sat on the edge of the tub, hugged myself, and stared at my shoes in an inch of overflowed water.

Because Susan insisted that I not call her Susan, I thought it only appropriate that she not call me Will. Soon we stopped answering each other's calls altogether. We simply let it ring twice, hung up, then let it ring twice again. That was our signal to meet at the doughnut shop across from Mesa Del Mar. We'd sit in pink plastic chairs and stare through the front window at German Shepherds doing sniff-searches of incoming students.

She would be Gail and I would be Tom and, to the rest of the world, we were married and had a townhouse. We spoke only in code. If she said, "I'm going to Africa tomorrow," it meant she'd be teaching school. The doughnut shop was "Home Base." Sam Perganov was "The Man." Surveillance was "The Radar." I wanted to refer to the things Susan ate at the doughnut shop as "The Poison," but I didn't dare. She sucked down crullers and cups of black coffee as if they were enchanted, some sort of mystic EMP-chaff that would keep her invisible as we sat and brooded and stared at our school.

Meanwhile, days passed in the wreckage of my apartment. I lived in the debris the way rats will after the last bomb drops and all that's left are piles of jagged concrete and twisted rebar sticking out of the ground. Sometimes, I laughed hysterically at the clogged toilet.

Out of mercy or sheer ineptitude, the ransackers had spared my computer and only bashed in the monitor. I immediately bought a new flat screen on credit so that, when I wasn't at the doughnut shop or doing super-slow gangster rolls past the front of Mesa Del Mar in my Land Rover, I could send Susan short emails Re: The Man in Africa. Was I falling in love with her? I wondered: were we sending each other mixed messages, or was it the real thing? There was no way to know. If you can't trust your phone lines and you don't have broadband, how can you trust your feelings? I wondered what code word I'd use if I had to say how I felt about her.

Good Sid, the born-again trucker, kept me company—a corpulent, stinking, latter-day Friar Tuck. We drank blessed Olympia Tumwater and watched the President get re-elected.

And, every night, I danced around my shattered bureau, did pirouettes between splintered holes in the floor, cooed sweet nothings to my hissing fridge. Sometimes, I laughed. Sometimes, I cried. I learned that the em dash should be replaced by a colon when preceding a formal clarifying or emphatic clause. I spent hours on *Amateur Hardcore Webcams* probing the nature of life. I ate my dinners watching riot police club protesters in the famed cities of antiquity. Nightsticks in Nasiriyah. Tear gas in Gifu. Bullets over Burgas.

Gail and Tom had their last doughnut rendezvous on a Sunday that felt like a Monday—the last day before Tom was supposed to go across the street to the Teacher's Conference Room and talk about his feelings. The Man in Africa demanded it: a psych evaluation that could be videotaped and sent to the parents of the browbeaten, traumatized strong safety currently nursing his delicate sensibilities in a small, yet restful, French château. If all went as planned and Tom showed the proper remorse for raising his voice, the parents would be satisfied enough to let their son return to the United States, would drop the remaining portion of their suit against the school district, and the boy would finish out the semester with a guaranteed B+ in the course. The Man would rehire Tom. All would be forgiven.

Across the street, the German Shepherds doing sniff-searches were, at that moment, making more than Tom. The air smelled like warm buttermilk.

"Do you realize those dogs . . ." said Tom, but Gail wasn't listening.

"Look at that car," she said, "the off-blue one. It drives past, what, like three or four times every time we're sitting here. Have you noticed that? Is that significant?"

Off-blue?

"Probably just a parent dropping a student off." I looked but none of the cars going by were blue. I hadn't once mentioned blue to Susan. How could she have known the relationship I had with that color? How could she? Could she? No one says "off-blue."

Tom tried to keep a straight face but, suddenly, he felt angry. Ugly, bitter insights sizzled across the brainpan.

"How could you do this to Tom?" I said. "How could you? Tom is very pissed."

"Has it occurred to you that you're not the most stable person?"

"Has it occurred to you, Gail, that Tom trusted you?"

She rolled her eyes and took a small bite of lethal cruller. But it was a telling bite, a studied bite, a bite far too measured even for the pretty and pouty of the world, who enjoy everything except Heinekens in the most proscribed amounts.

"I don't think I can hang out with you anymore," she said to her coffee.

"Your bite betrays you," I said, "just as you've betrayed me. You've been working for him all along, haven't you? And all this time I thought we had something."

"We have nothing." She took another bite, bigger this

time, and squinted at the distant football team scrimmaging on the upper field—minus, of course, our strong safety, who was busy rebuilding his emotional security over *Celery Rémoulade* and *Crème Brûlée.*

"You're nothing but a tool for The Man," I said.

She was a henchwoman, a hypocrite, a desperada trying to hold onto her lousy job. So desperate, in fact, that she'd gone undercover for Sam Perganov just to find out if I was a problem.

Susan looked at me. "You've got a problem," she said, "that needs professional attention."

I blinked. The whole world, for the briefest instant, had gone completely blue.

I didn't know a damn thing about any tunnels.

I would have said as much to my psych evaluator, but he didn't ask me whether I'd seen *The Battle of Algiers*, whether I could do the handshake. He didn't mention rioters in Japan, or pollution in the water and how it made me feel.

He merely turned on the video camera behind him and asked, "Would you mind an implant?"

"An implant?"

"A small one." My psych evaluator smiled. His name was Mel, and he had the broad American smile of Masons and ministers. People in the Massachusetts Bay Colony had that smile, and in Salem, and the Ohio River Valley, and at the Alamo.

"What does it do?"

"You'll never know it's there."

"But how come I'd want one?"

"You don't want to be left behind, do you? It's cutting edge."

We looked at each other, but silence seemed to make Mel uneasy. He drummed his fingers on the table, loosened his tie.

"It's nothing. It's next to nothing. You won't even think about it. It monitors the pH in your skin to give us a general sense of how you're feeling. And it helps us find you in emergencies. Harmless. I'm not kidding."

He took off his watch and showed me a faint dime-shaped bruise on the underside of his wrist. "That's it," he said. "It's that simple."

"Simple." I felt cold and thought of Cantonese lobster, thought of making a break for the door.

Mel took my right hand firmly in both of his and flashed me a winning smile. "You know why I'm so happy, Will? I used to get enraged. I used to get completely out of control. But now, if some guy gets in my face, some—person—thinks he's too good for what I have to offer, know what I do?"

"No."

"Not a damn thing. I don't get angry." He let go and put his feet up on the table, mopped his forehead with the back of his sleeve, then looked down at his belly and smiled. "The district sends out a troubleshooter, and I sit back and take it easy. It really is that simple."

He said the implants would soon be standard issue for all high school teachers throughout the state, but right now the focus was on English and art. Speech, drama, philosophy, and history teachers were strongly encouraged. "College professors, on the other hand," he whispered, "are a whole different thing."

Did I agree to the implant because I was afraid that if I didn't Mel would come across the table and bite out my trachea or blind me with his thumbs? Maybe. I wondered if some of Mel's troubleshooters had already troubleshot the inside of my apartment.

"I'm a team player," I said, clenching my fist under the table.

"I knew you were," said Mel.

Later, I'd stop telling people anything at all. I'd give up the single life for Ethical Abstinence and leave dating cruises for the balding French. And, yes, I'd get my old job back.

It didn't take long before I found Jesus and realized that that was Sid's motive for coming over all along. It all goes back to the Tumwater, I guess. Sitting in my living room, farting and belching with Sid to the CNN loop, I watched our President smile the good smile, and I realized that we *were* in a stronger America; Jesus loved us; and the half-dead fern hanging over the breakfast nook wasn't actually recording me.

The rows of Olympia cans in my new hissless fridge gleam when I open the door. Their very presence testifies to my goodness. I open the fridge and say, "Testify," and in some parallel universe where America is right and free and no longer threatened by the slavering unwashed hordes beyond its borders, they answer me: "Amen, brother."

And Susan Thorrson? She met a bad end. They caught her on tape doing something illegal but no one knows what. It's not my business. Justice will prevail.

"Here it comes," says Sid, "the *Apo-ca-lypse*." Some kind of new uranium-based weapons system being tested outside of Reno. We both laugh hysterically for as long as we can.

Call Me Mr. Lucky

Sue Wagner hated me. She wrote me anonymous notes in red marker. *Nothing You Say Will Ever Be True Because You Will Never Be Honest*. She emailed me obscure riddles: "What do the Koi care for algebra? For that matter, what do the sharks?," "To the robin in the cage, why the color of dawn?," "The conversation was dead, but who heard it die?" There was nothing I could do to stop her.

In the morning, the tall windows of the bank would be filled with inky darkness unique to San Diego, thick and impenetrable, fading into late-morning haze and then hard, clear sun. I'd get to work early—but not as early as Sue—and see her sitting at her desk across the bank, looking at me, wearing the indigo hawk mask salvaged from last year's Halloween party. The eyes were punched-out ovals. A purple plume stuck up from the back of the head. As soon as someone else would come in, she'd take it off. But when it was just us: the mask and her penetrating stare.

It was my first year in San Diego. And enough had happened in that year to make me nervous. I'd come from an assistant manager position at the Cedar Rapids branch, thin and edgy, used to working 10-hour days and melting down my nights in the Philosopher's Club over drinks and loneliness. Not the most healthy lifestyle, I know. Still, what you do in the Midwest is not what you do in California. Now that I had moved, I was eating better. I'd started doing push-ups. But

91

once you're edgy, I mean deeply, structurally edgy, it sticks with you. On top of that, I met and married a sitcom writer named Diana in the course of several weeks after I got out West. And I loved that woman—even though we started to argue almost immediately and I moved out of her apartment three or four days after moving in. I'm not proud of it, but my feelings were genuine.

Sue Wagner knew all this somehow. She intuited it, saw it feathered over me like dust. And she hated me even more because she felt that she understood me. I was not better. I was not more efficient. I was an edgy guy from Cedar Rapids, and *she* knew about *Cedar Rapids*. I was that much more of a fraud because I came from the Midwest. We had the same skills. She probably knew even more than I did about managing a bank. And it burned her ass, juggling all that together. Sue Wagner had a burned ass and a bad attitude. Even without the hawk mask, I could see it on her face.

But forget all that. That comes later. Forget my emotional isolation. And the bad judgment, born of such isolation, drunk and horny at the Halloween party in the copy room with a teller named Kiesha, up against a double stack of HB-Bond Xerographic paper, it's too soon to bring that up. Or how to get rid of Kiesha after that, designed to camouflage the real yawning inconsistencies of my life. All of that can wait.

What's important right now is that Sue Wagner hated me, and wanted my job. That much was clear. I'd been brought in from outside. She was in line, and I'd stepped right in front of her. As assistant manager, I was a minor lord of a minor fief. And I ruled the tellers with an even hand.

The manager, Hollace White, was my only superior. He came in once or twice a week, looking faintly managerial, and made very few decisions. This made both of us happy. He stayed out of my hair. My loyal subjects were calm and efficient. No one stole from the till, and the tellers usually balanced at the end of the day. But Sue had a fire in her belly that wasn't going out, despite my benevolence. And, given what Hollace White had just asked me to do, hot shit was about to hit the fan with Sue Wagner.

I was standing by the vault with a paper cup full of

lousy coffee the janitor had made the night before. My hands were shaking, so I didn't look at the cup. I tried not to look at Sue, either. It was time for the yearly inventory, the only thing we did at the bank that had nothing directly to do with money. It meant counting the transport bags, coin-rolling papers, deposit envelopes, release forms, morning intake forms, overflow forms, hundreds of forms, office supplies, rubber bands, everything. It was like a spring cleaning, and it meant overtime, hours of overtime, and nobody wanted a second shift.

This is how it worked. Hollace White had clout because he never told anyone to do anything. He was hardly there. So, when he *did* speak, he was God, and I was his prophet. He didn't *tell* me to do it. The day before, he'd called me into his office and *asked* me like we were best friends: "Mike, you think you could *rustle up* some yearly inventory tomorrow night?" Well, sure I could. I'd be delighted to. I didn't have a problem with that. I was looking forward to it.

And then it was up to me. No more benevolence: if I came off as too benevolent, everyone would laugh in my face, and I'd be there all night, tallying bill slips and trash can liners. I had to coerce somebody to do it with me, bully them into it and, unfortunately, the only people available were Sue Wagner and Bill Jones. One of them would have to give.

Granted, this is what I got paid to do, what Hollace meant by *rustling up*. But he knew and I knew that *rustling* was going to be hard in this case. And I wasn't looking forward to spending extra hours with my masked admirer. So I went over to Bill Jones first.

Bill was youngish forties—say forty-one or two with something like racquetball or tennis keeping his belly down. He had sandy brown hair, cut conservatively, and favored white Oxford shirts pressed to creases. I watched him from a distance as if studying his habits would make me a better hunter. But you can only learn so many things from how a person counts out money, and most of those things I already knew, at least in Bill's case. He was fastidious and precise. He had a good sense of rhythm with his hands. He was probably fast enough to pocket a twenty here and there. And he didn't, which meant he was honest. Furthermore, he knew I was on the swoop, about to talk to him, and that was a problem.

Bill, himself, was a problem, an ongoing problem, because he was smarter than me, and we both knew it. Whenever I would walk over to his teller window, radiating my low-grade feudal benevolence, he would blend in with the carpet, take immediate, evasive action. Bill Jones had the ability to stretch out a meeting with a customer or vanish into thin air. Whenever I had a task to assign, he'd be involved in something else. And he always looked busy. When you know an employee has these skills, you know you're dealing with a veteran, somebody who can see you coming. And Bill had me pegged the minute I set my coffee down.

I stood behind him, already smiling, and waited for him to finish with a customer. There was no one else in his line. I'd timed it so that there wasn't much more he could do to stretch the transaction out. The customer walked away. I could sense desperation rolling off of him in waves.

"Bill," I grinned, pumping his hand with both of mine, "how are things?"

"Things?"

"Yeah, you know, wife and kid, that hobby—what was that hobby you do? Building ships in bottles?"

"They work." By *they work*, I didn't know if he meant that his wife and kid have jobs or that they work well in his life. I wasn't sure and felt a moment of panic when I realized that it was another teller who built model ships in bottles, not Bill Jones.

"That's great." I nodded and smiled. He broke into a thin, watery smile and nodded as well, searching his peripheral vision for another customer to get him out of this.

"So you know we're doing inventory tomorrow night. Nothing too drastic. Just a few hours. And I can't very well be here all by myself."

A new customer was now standing at the end of the velvet-roped stanchions in the middle of the bank, and Bill kept trying to turn toward her. But I blocked all eye contact.

"So what do you say to a little extra cash?"

And then, Bill Jones turned invisible: "Well, I'd love to,

Mike, but my son just had a major operation, and I have to go pick him up from the hospital because the wife's out of town." He turned toward the customer. "Can I can help you?"

It sounded pre-recorded—a special tape he played in desperate situations like this. My entire attack had been deflected. How do you bully someone with a son in the hospital and a wife out of town? I went back to my desk and put my face in my hands. Bill Jones was James Bond, and there was only Sue Wagner left.

That morning, Sue had left me a note that read, *You Wouldn't Feel Ashamed If You Didn't Feel Guilty.* I walked over and sat down in one of the brown upholstered chairs in front of her desk. She was working on the daily balance sheet for the entire bank—my job, actually. I had already done it, but Sue was fond of re-doing things I had already done.

"Well," I said. "So."

She looked up at me as if it was the first time in her life she'd ever heard dog shit speak, then went back to her figures. Her desk calculator ticked. She punched the numbers with the point of her pen like she hated the buttons. Sue had shoulder-length, brown hair and, at the right angle, she didn't look too bad. But she was crazy, and crazy cancelled everything else out.

"I'll do it," she said.

"Do what?"

"What you've come to ask me to do." She gave me an icy smile.

"How do you know what I've come to ask you to do?"

"Well, are you asking?"

"I might be asking."

"Then I'll do it."

"What if I was asking you to go jump off a bridge or stick that pen through your hand?"

"You want me to stick this pen through my hand?"

"No, but what if that's what I was asking?"

"Then I'd say, you do it." She put the pen down in front of me and spread her hand on the desk like a starfish. We looked at each other.

"Inventory," I said. "Tomorrow night."

"Great. You still want to stick this pen through my hand?" She still had her cold little smile.

Maybe it was that smile that did it. But, after work, I drove out to see my wife. Even though we'd only been together for a short time, even though she'd kicked me out, Diana was still my wife. And that meant privileges. She had to at least talk to me. I don't know; I was still in love. I could be romantic. I hadn't given up hope. And I knew that before there was a breeze again, before the days got much cooler, she'd be gone. She'd go up to LA for a while for work, and that would be it.

I pressed my cheek against the mint-painted door to her study and listened. The inside of her apartment had always reminded me of mint ice-cream trimmed with vanilla. The door frames and the edges of the ceilings had yellowed over the years from the dust and smoke of renters. Now, they were the dull off-white of true vanilla. And the mint paint, chipped in places, showed white in its pocks, as if some of the vanilla trimming had broken off and was drifting through the pale green.

The door was cold, as was everything in the apartment, which was the way Diana liked it—cold and clean and minimal. She never got the sniffles. She'd had two flus in the last five years. Diana was immune to everything. And, especially during the hot months, she kept the AC cranked up to maximum blast. I shut my eyes and listened to her Ticonderoga scratch across a yellow steno pad. She was the loudest writer in the world. She pressed so hard, gripped her pencil so tightly, that, for a time, she'd had to wear a brace on her hand. During one of our arguments, I told her she should be an engraver, not a sitcom writer. But none of that mattered now. Not the arguments. Not whoever she was sleeping with in LA. Not my feeble attempts with an obsessive college girl named Amanda. I could put all that behind me. Even getting kicked out. I didn't own much. It was enough for me just to listen to that pencil scratch and feel the cold paint against my cheek.

I'd taken off my shoes downstairs and slipped in

through the circular window over the sink that didn't lock and slid upwards on its sash. I'd accidentally stepped on some dishes under an inch of dirty water, and I left wet footprints up the stairs. I still had my key, but I was afraid to use the door in case Diana had changed the locks, clicking yet another obstacle in place between us.

She cleared her throat. I heard the crinkle of a sheet being lifted and set on what I knew was a stack of yellow sheets covered with script. Diana was a creature of habit. She couldn't write well without her pencils and steno pads, a burning cigarette in the ashtray, and the cold.

I spread my palms against the door as Sue Wagner had done earlier on her desk—two pale starfish. Soon Diana would have to drive up to LA. She'd told me all about it once. Since she'd kicked me out, I'd watched both of her shows religiously. She would have already written the first five episodes of *The Dog* and *Yes, We Are Open*. She'd have to meet with the directors and casts to talk about the next five. And then she'd disappear for at least a month, possibly more, into LA's maze of pass gates and access codes, exclusive restaurants and unlisted numbers. She probably had a boyfriend up there. It wouldn't have shocked me to find that out. I was ready for it. But you never know. You have to play the odds. And, in spite of Sue Wagner and the inventory waiting for me like a shot of bad medicine I didn't want to take, I told myself I was lucky. Playing the odds doesn't always mean you have to lose.

"Open the door," she said, "and tell me what you want." Just like that. Flat. Monotone. Not giving anything up.

I swung the door slowly inwards, and there she was, brown hair dull and unwashed, piercing gray eyes, a thin line of smoke clawing up from the corner of the desk. Her hands were folded on top of an old, stained blotter. And, of course, nothing was out of place. The books that covered each wall were arranged by thickness and height, virgin steno pads stacked exactly flush with the corner of the table behind her. There was some sort of abstract painting between the bookcases.

"Yes?" she said. "Explain to me how you're not breaking and entering." Diana had her cell phone nearby at all times with 911 on speed dial. She didn't have to punch the three digits or even turn it on. She could just hit a button, and the SDPD would come wailing down the street. As far as I knew, she'd never used it like that. But she might. On me.

"It's been, what, three weeks? Four weeks?" I walked over and sat in the single studded-leather armchair, placed directly facing her writing desk—suggesting interrogation more than comfort. I wondered who had sat here recently. I wondered who would want to. And I couldn't shake the *déjà vu* of having sat in front of Sue Wagner's desk that morning. Granted, I didn't think Diana was sick in the head like Sue. But there were too many correspondences for my taste, and it put me even more on edge.

"Don't be ridiculous," said Diana. "It's been a million years, and I don't know you. I don't want to know you."

"I thought I might have left some things." I said.

"I changed the locks. You used the window." She took a black plastic gun with a metal prong sticking out of the barrel from a drawer. "I keep this with me now. For unexpected visitations."

"Have I ever threatened you?"

"No, *I'm* threatening *you*."

"I just wanted to talk."

"This is a stun gun. It'll deliver fifty thousand volts of electricity down a wire when I fire it into you."

"Would you like that?"

"I might enjoy it. I won't enjoy cleaning up after you. But, no rose without the thorn, right?"

"I don't know why it has to be like this." I leaned forward and took a menthol light out of the pack on her desk but hesitated, holding the flame of my lighter in front of the cigarette.

"If you light that, I shoot."

We stared at each other. Then she grinned cruelly, but I felt okay. I really wasn't worried. She'd been my wife. That still counted for something. I exhaled.

"Jesus," I said, "you can't be serious." I took a long draw on the cigarette, and she shot me in the chest.

Later, when I came to on the sidewalk, outside the long,

white, block-length wall of windows and doorways that was the complex, I found a note in my pocket. But it took me a few minutes before I could think straight enough to comprehend what was written on it. Yes, I'd pissed myself but, luckily, it hadn't been any more embarrassing than that. I had the worst headache of my life. My teeth were buzzing. My arm was cut from her dragging me out, and I could taste blood in my mouth. I leaned against the apartment complex and dry heaved for a while. The note read:

> *Wallet mailed to your place just for fun — expect it in a few days. Left you your keys but took my old one back. I'm off to LA. Don't bother me again. And fuck you.*

I looked up and down the street. Diana's blue Miata was gone. When I got into my car, I checked my eyes in the rear-view mirror. They were bloodshot as hell, nerves all over my body twitching, and I still felt like throwing up. She'd shot me with that thing, and I'd never raised a hand toward her or threatened to once. I wasn't the violent type. I drove home slowly, unsteadily, and sat for a while in the ripped maroon Barcalounger I'd bought at a yard sale. I wanted to run a bath, but I was afraid of water at the moment, my nerves sending little shots of pain all over my body. I had visions of myself blown through the bathroom tile, my skin blackened like dinner gone wrong. So I called Amanda instead.

Amanda. She had a cat named Junior and, on her answering machine, she meowed and pretended to be him. She was twenty years old and the one affair I'd ever had on the one woman who'd blasted me with a stun gun. Everything about Amanda had been a mistake, and I hadn't called her in a while. Still, I needed sympathy. I heard the beep and said, "Amanda, I've been electrocuted by my wife. I don't know how long I've got. Call me." Wife plus death probably meant a prompt call back in Amanda's voice — not Junior's — which would have been nice, considering the fact that she only spoke to me now through the cat. She'd say, *Junie says I should ask you to dinner*, or, *Junior, go ask daddy to get mommy a glass of water.* There was only so much of that I could take.

She didn't call back, and I sat by the phone all night, nervously jiggling my leg up and down, thinking about explosions and what food in my fridge would have a damping instead of a conducting effect.

The next day was heavy drama and customers in my face, too much coffee, jangling nerves, and side glances from Sue every few minutes. I knew I had to keep it together. I knew my people looked to me for a stable, guiding presence. So I stood in the vault a lot, working on not thinking about angry wives and voltage, drinking cup after cup of poison coffee, and pretending I was in *The Dog*.

The show's premise: sweater-wearing white guy from Boston runs all-night greasy spoon in East LA. Colorful-yet-endearing gang members. Bumbling-yet-endearing LAPD regulars. Moralizing about racial-ethnic tolerance usually worked in by the end of each episode. Endless mileage from Boston accent versus LA hood slang. Laughter in all the right places. No one in *The Dog* ever got smoked with a stun gun. Maybe that's why I liked the show—no danger of anyone waking up as a human lightning rod with a note in his pocket.

"Excuse me?" One of the tellers. Gracelia. A very sweet, meek little woman, originally from Honduras, who wore emerald green business suits and ate enough candy in a day to kill a regular person. "Hello there. Are you okay?"

I spun, almost spilling acid French Roast on the vault's Kelly green linoleum. "Of course I'm okay. Don't I look okay?"

"Well, I just thought I'd ask, you see, because Ellis Stearnes is here—"

"And he wants to see his box."

She nodded, wincing, as if *Ellis Stearnes* was code for *hit me in the face now, please*.

"Okay." I handed her the coffee and straightened my tie. "Okay. No problem. Thank you." And I glided gracefully out of the vault, chock-full of capable, managerial *savoir-faire*. I think I was still partly in *The Dog* because I might have started to affect a Boston accent. But that didn't matter. The point is,

I suddenly pulled it together; I got myself going because, at least with Ellis Stearnes, I knew what I was up against.

Of course, Sue Wagner was bustling around the edges of my vision like a dead moon radiating spiritual darkness. And I had to consciously avoid thinking about doing inventory that night and what it would mean if she put on the indigo hawk mask as soon as it was just us. But Ellis Stearnes was irate enough—dependably irate enough—that I suddenly had gray matter between my ears again and a solvable problem in front of me.

Ellis Stearnes wasn't Texan, but he pretended to be. And what he lacked in big, Southern bluster, he made up for in meanness. He had a thick face that looked worked-over with a pumice—a desert rock hit by too much wind and sand. He scowled at me as I walked up.

"Hello, and how are you?" I held out my hand and gave him a wide, I've-been-counting-the-days-since-the-last-time-you-came-in smile.

"Look. Let's go. And you can cut the shit, boy, because I'm just here to see my box."

"Wonderful. Right. Okay," I said as he crossed his arms and squared off, squinting at me. "I have my key right here. And, if you have yours, we can go right this way."

"No shit I have my key. What do you take me for, goddammit."

That sort of talk was a given. The women wouldn't deal with him because he'd call them *little lady* and tell them they'd do better at the Mustang Ranch with their legs in the air or something like that. Or maybe he wouldn't say anything at all and just glare at them like he was about to slap them silly. I took him to the side room off the vault where the safety deposit boxes were, and we unlocked his.

Unlike with most of our customers, I knew what Ellis Stearnes kept in his box because it weighed at least two hundred pounds, and neither of us could lift it by ourselves. Any time a box was that heavy, it had metal in it, lots of metal. And that meant coins. I guessed gold or silver dollars, given that Stearnes wore them all over his body. He had them in his belt, the band of his cowboy hat, hanging around his neck on a gold chain or in a bolo tie.

We clinked the box down in a viewing booth, and he glowered at me as I walked away, waiting until he thought I was out of earshot before he opened it up. He liked to sit in the viewing booth and run his fingers over the coins, cooing to himself as if he were stroking the hair of a sick child. He came in to do this about once every two weeks, and we'd all gotten over snickering at him for it.

Half an hour later, he was still in the viewing booth, and I looked up from some paperwork to find Sue Wagner standing over me.

"Stearnes just buzzed," she said. When a customer was finished viewing the contents of a box, there was a red button to push so a bank employee could come and put the box back. I stood.

"Let me go. I'll handle it," she said, raising her eyebrows and nodding.

"Yeah?"

"Are you going to tell me I can't?"

"Weren't you the one who said people like him should be castrated for their own good?" I hadn't noticed it before, but now I heard Stearnes laying on the buzzer.

"He's getting angry," she said.

"Be my guest." I sat back down and watched Sue stalk towards the vault, her light gray slacks swishing as she walked. Taking a sip of cold coffee, I waited for all hell to break loose.

But it didn't. And that was more unnerving than any outburst. Sue Wagner was in there for less than two minutes and, to this day, I have no idea what she said to him. But he came out first, a soft, bewildered look on his face—almost an apologetic look—and she strolled behind with a quiet little smirk.

"He's a sweet, sweet little man," she said as she passed my desk, and I felt suddenly cold. Sue was unbreakable. Sue could turn piss into lemonade.

The thought of spending hours with her, cleaning the bank, made me run back in the vault and stare at the glistening, Kelly green linoleum.

An hour before closing, I left the bank and took a drive. The inventory with Sue was right in front of me, and it felt like the night before my execution. I stopped at a supermarket and bought a large pink bottle of Pepto-Bismol, a case of beer, and three pack of menthols, Marlboros, Diana's brand. Then I parked by the beach for a while and looked at the water. Maybe it was the coffee or a stray volt still forking in my stomach, but I felt shaky, a little ill.

I'd planned to get good and sauced, to ride the evening out pleasantly numb, but I wound up depressed, sipping Pepto out of a paper bag as if it were Thunderbird, and brooding about my wife in Los Angeles. We'd met in the bank, of course, when she came in to open a new account. Now, she banked somewhere else. The day she closed her account, she said, "This isn't working for me"—the same thing she said the morning she piled all my possessions on the curb. The bank's karma and my own seemed linked, and the only place I could relax was the vault. I wondered what Hollace would say if I put a cot in there. I drained the Pepto and put the car in reverse.

On my way back, I went to a magic shop and bought a rubber Richard Nixon mask. If she was going to be a hawk all night, I'd be Tricky Dick. I'd be ready.

The inventory proved to be a dirty job, dirtier than either of us had expected.

At 10:30 we'd completed over half of it in utter silence.

The sidewalk outside was lit up with the lemon-white sodium glow of streetlights and, from the interior of the bank, the concrete looked creamy orange. Sue and I faced the giant crate of deposit canisters that used to go in the old-fashioned vacuum-tube drive-ups. ATMs had made the canisters obsolete, but Hollace liked a clean bank. So into the storage hallway we went.

It was congested and musty, rat pellets on the floor and the paraphernalia of forty years of banking stacked haphazardly up to the ceiling. We air-blasted the canisters until we got sick with dust, scrubbed the floors, threw out tons of useless paper that previous inventories had conveniently overlooked. It took the rest of the night, but we cleaned and counted everything in the entire bank, communicating in monosyllables, sometimes only grunting.

When we finished, the streetlights had gone off, and the windows were glossy black with morning darkness.

I went out to my car and brought in the beer.

"Here," I said and handed her a can. Sue looked like a raccoon, clean circles around her eyes where she'd worn goggles air-blasting the hallway.

"I don't think so." She set the can down and looked at me.

"Oh no?"

"No."

"What, then? Hawk mask? Fucked-up haiku?"

Her mouth twitched. She went over to her desk and put on the hawk mask, then came back and opened the beer. "It's better this way," she said. "Isn't it?"

Tricky Dick's face was thin latex, and I had it wadded up in my pocket. I pulled it out, and it popped perfectly into shape. We blinked at each other through our respective eye holes, lifting up the bottoms of our masks to take sips of beer. In a way, it was easier.

"How about this," I said. "If life is a prison, then where are the bars?"

"No. If life is a prison, then who are the guards?"

I nodded and thought for a while. "The temperature was dropping, but where would it land?"

"If love is a sword, how sharp is the edge?" She set her empty can down and we looked at each other in silence, expressionless in our masks. We were standing against the long tellers' counter that ran the length of the bank. For the first time, I noticed that this part of the bank was mostly dark, only small service lights on over the vault and the storage hallway.

I put my beer down, too, and got up close to the beak of her mask, grasped her shoulders, and ran my hands down the sides of her arms. In the eye holes of her mask, Sue's eyes were light hazel, the pupils large. She had changed into jeans and a T-shirt at some point before closing, and my hands slid over the stiff belt loops, the pockets.

"I have to go," she said and turned quickly—walking, then running towards the exit.

I ran after her, tripping over small end tables and plush gray chairs that were hard to see in the dark with the mask on. She was better running in a mask than me, and she made it to her car by the time I was just reaching the side door. I stood on the sidewalk. Me: an apparition of President Nixon in khakis, my face twisted slightly to the side, watching an indigo hawk lay smoke and rubber into early morning traffic.

When I got to my apartment, I sat immediately in the maroon Barcalounger, gripping the armrests tightly; the voltage was still in there, toying with me. A red number one was blinking on the answering machine. I watched it blink on and off for a long time, putting the Nixon mask on, then taking it off, then putting in back on again. Finally, with the mask on, I played the message. It was from Amanda, telling me her cat had decided we weren't right for each other, but that Junior hoped I was okay. I threw the answering machine against the wall and stomped it to pieces.

Covered in dust, my hair looked like it had gone gray overnight. My shirt looked like it had been in an explosion. I cut a hole in Nixon's lips so I could smoke through the mask while I roped the Barcalounger down in the trunk of my car. Through the open passenger window, I tossed in the beer, some grapefruit, a bunch of bananas, T-shirts and underwear, my microwave, and my Louisville Slugger—signed by Pete Rose before his public disgrace. Then I wrapped a blanket around myself and peeled out for the Big LA to find the woman I loved before the lightning in my body turned my brain into a small, exploding star.

Death and Texas

Could it be the Lethe that spills out below Joe's house, rushing up underground from hidden veins connected to New Orleans' canals and then back, around the house's wooden and concrete foundation, masquerading as a rivulet of the Mississippi?

Perhaps.

It will never be known how this could have happened. Knowledge is memory, and Lethe destroys memory, making the giant rats fat in the canals. It swells the cockroaches to ten times their normal size, causing them to forget what it is to be cockroaches. And cockroaches who can't even remember how to be cockroaches are easy prey for the rats, who, since before the time of Napoleon, have feared the Mississippi. Maybe this is because, at one time, they all knew that the Mississippi could become the Lethe. Maybe, at one time, the Styx, Cocytus, or Acheron came through.

But this is conjecture.

That the emergence of Lethe in New Orleans' Garden District will *never* be remembered and, therefore, could never have been known, is difficult. It is a problem for Joe, who must now step over its smoking waters in order to leave his house. I know nothing, thinks Joe, not yet able to grasp the irony of such a conclusion as he stands in his front yard, wondering why water is spilling out from a small fissure beneath his front steps.

Meanwhile, Joe is having other difficulties. Everything is happening at once.

Take his house: empty, not a thing in it but carpet. Joe tells himself he likes it like that, though only last week, his psychiatrist, Trent, accused him of being too cheap to buy a bed. And romance: Joe has just discovered that his ex-girlfriend has bugged his light fixtures.

His house is minimal—there's a refrigerator, a toilet, a coffee maker, oscillating fans, and a gas stove so covered in dust that it will burn if he ever turns it on. The carpet smells like old rubber . . . and the waters of the Lethe. It's a simple house, a small mint stucco with cracks, on Decatur Street, surrounded by Spanish moss in the trees. Of course, there are also the cameras.

Across the street, his ex-girlfriend, Sharon, watches him through tiny video cameras hidden in the lights. There are three: one in the living room, one in the bedroom, and one in the bathroom. He found them two days ago. She'd probably tap the phone if he had a phone. Ceramic wall mic? Whisper dish? Shotgun microphone aimed at his front door? Joe knows all of these are possible. Joe knows Sharon is capable of that and more. The light bulb in the living room popped, and when he got up on a footstool to change it, he saw the miniature black lens as big as a cap eraser. The simultaneous emergence of the Lethe and the cameras is a coincidence too staggering to contemplate.

Sharon is inventive. She's smart and obsessive. She's got a lot of money—Texas money, daddy money—and that means she can do things like bug her ex-boyfriend's house and sit there at the monitor, eating Chinese food from Joyous Wok. Joe has seen it. She's been renting the apartment across the street and parks her rouge Audi TT three blocks away. He noticed it once on his nightly walk to Dairy Queen. He saw it from a distance, then snuck through the alley and up to the side window of the apartment. There she was: white Joyous Wok carton and chopsticks in hand, syrupy country music playing, monitor randomly cycling through the camera views.

He'd asked her to marry him, on impulse, after sex

early one morning in her canopy bed. And she gave him a deep, emotive *yes* that instantly made him think of ravens flying over empty rooftops, the distant Cathleen of funeral bells, old European prisons, the bottom of the ocean. He said: "Or maybe we should just think about it, maybe, as a possibility sometime in the far possible future." But she said *yes*, again, the same way. She started making plans, dropped out of Tulane, spent nights in his bed or in a sleeping bag in his living room if he said he wanted space. After a while, she only went back to her place to do laundry.

He made noises: "Look. I need even more space. Suffocating. I don't know what I want. I finally know what I want. I need to go. We'll talk later. I don't think it would be good for us to talk. Take care of yourself. Be good to yourself. It's me, not you."

She made noises: "How could you do this? Only you could do this. If you really loved me. All this time. You never loved me. Promises you made. Liar. Everything I did for you. I hate you. I loved you. You're a bastard. Never again. Call me?"

She went home and sat on her canopy bed and cried. He sat on the carpet in his mint stucco house and hated himself.

Now he's lying spread-eagled in the middle of his living room floor, reading about parakeets. Joe imagines himself spread-eagled on her monitor screen. He imagines her eating out of a white Joyous Wok carton with chopsticks.

Joe does not need to work and, normally, he doesn't; he inherited enough money from a rich uncle to be fixed up for the rest of his natural life. But, on the advice of his psychiatrist, he teaches "Introduction to Meditation" once a week, on Wednesday afternoons, to idle housewives and thin, hairless men on Social Security. It's supposed to give him direction, perspective, help him prioritize.

Summer in New Orleans means the humidity is close to 100 percent. But the Reily Student Recreation Center is crisp and cool. Joe's students breathe deeply on blue floor mats. Their eyes are closed. The ones who can manage to sit in the lotus position, do. The others do their best. Joe stands above them in baggy sweats and a Seattle Mariners T-shirt.

"All eyes are closed," he says. "All heads are bowed."

Mr. Jenkins has started to moan—as he always does before meditating. He's the oldest one, almost ninety, and when he breathes deeply, his nostrils suck in like gills.

"Gloria, close your eyes and focus." Gloria Riddel has to sit in a folding chair because getting up and down is too difficult for a woman of her size. She leers at Joe from the back of the room. Her husband, Byron, a very large, red-faced man in pinstripes, has begun to come to class with her. Byron doesn't believe in meditation. He doesn't close his eyes. He glares at Joe.

Joe repeats phrases taken from the meditation book his psychiatrist lent him: "Today, we have resolved to become more of who we already are. Today is the day of our awakening. Now is the moment of our realization with the moment."

Mr. Jenkins breathes loudly. Tom Polehaus, a middle-aged tractor salesman from Baton Rouge, sits erect in the full lotus, eyes closed, a wide, peaceful smile on his face. Young, pretty Michelle DuPont seems as if she is about to cry.

Joe's students are an emotional bunch, most of whom are taking this summer class for reasons that have nothing to do with learning to meditate. Which is a good thing, thinks Joe, because *I don't know how.*

"With every breath, we let in relaxation and let out tension. With every breath, we let in an expanding awareness of this unique moment in space and time."

Last week, Michelle stood up and spontaneously confessed the affair she was having on her husband. Joe looks at her and then at his four other students, wondering how long it will be before Mr. Jenkins collapses from exhaustion or there is another outburst or someone stands and declares a humiliating secret and leaves for good. At the beginning of the class, Joe had twenty students. Now he has five.

"Today," says Joe, "we'll be working on the Laughing Meditation." Joe has worried about this. The text calls for "a liberation of one's attachment to the immediate constraints of the physical through the catharsis of laughing." They were supposed to try it at home first.

"Now, let's start laughing." Joe does his best to set an example as he walks around the room: short, staccato barks of laughter—HA-HA-HA-HA. Tom Polehaus summons up a HEE-HEE-HO-HEH-HO, little laughs rising like air bubbles to the surface. It reminds Joe of jingle bells. Michelle is already sobbing. And Mr. Jenkins peals out heavy, cigarette-stripped, old-man guffaws—HAW-HAW-HAW-HAW-HAW—as if he were striking the air with his voice.

"Yes," says Joe, "yes, free yourself through laughter, HAHA."

Gloria Riddel is laughing now, eyes closed, belly quivering under her muumuu. Byron, is not laughing, however. He glares at Joe with his arms crossed, sweating into his button-down despite the air conditioning.

Joe walks up and stands in front of him: "HAHAHA?"

Byron channels as much hostility as possible into his glare, purses his lips.

Joe keeps laughing, his HAs sounding more like coughs, until Mr. Jenkins starts to choke on his own laughter. On the mat behind the old man, Michelle DuPont has curled up into the fetal position to weep.

"You're doing great," yells Joe and eventually asks them to stop. But the laughing continues, and Mr. Jenkins has to lie down.

Regarding mythological rivers, what can one say? Joe's calls to Water & Power are inconclusive, the voices on the other end indifferent: "A smoking river you say? Hmm. We don't show anything like that in your area." "There haven't been any other calls to this effect. Is the water very high?" "I'm sorry, this sounds like a question for 'Canals and Drains'— which would be extension 4721. Would you like me to transfer you there?" Eventually, Canals and Drains promises to send someone out. This, however, is not a solution. In the wee hours of the morning, Joe looks out a side window and sees a rat as big as a mailbox.

What makes strangeness strange, thinks Joe staring at chemical rainbows glittering on the surface of the pool below his front steps, is its closeness to the un-strange. Fact: the rats are abnormally large. But, in all fairness, insects and assorted vermin in Louisiana have always been oversized due to the humidity. Fact: the water is cloudy—fogged as if two parts river were mixed with one part milk—and it smokes. On the other hand, Joe heard a story of a polluted lake near Pittsburgh that actually caught on fire when someone pitched a cigarette into it. Fact: since the waters came forth, he has been having dreams of gigantic parakeets flying up out of fissures in the earth; he has been dreaming that the constellations have been changing places in the sky. But Joe's *Complete Book on Spiritual Astrology* has assured him that, throughout history, there have been many astral phenomena that are still unexplained by traditional Western science.

Added to this, Joe has been feeling dull. He is unsure whether the flooded foundation is not emitting some fume that is making him slow. It is possible, he thinks, that I am imagining all of this. But, then, isn't that *always* a possibility? Joe is afraid for his mind, though he practices good mental hygiene by constantly reading and remaining open to new experiences— which is a pretty good argument against stupefaction. In the last year, Joe has read *The Letters of Vincent van Gogh, Ancient Myths, The Odyssey, Death on the Installment Plan, The Selected Poems of Rainer Maria Rilke, The Last Whole Earth Catalog,* and *Human, All Too Human.* Now he is reading *A Field Guide to Aviculture.* Joe has many interests. He has considered getting a yellow Labrador. He has considered building a model railroad in the guest bedroom. He has considered television. Not local or cable but a gigantic satellite hook-up with five thousand channels so he can watch crop reports in Korea and South African talk shows. Joe has considered learning the languages of the shows he might watch.

But, for now, library books. Whatever is in the "New Arrivals" section is fair game. He finds himself staring blankly into the light fixture when his arms get tired of holding up his book. He finds himself thinking of Sharon and of aviculture. Sometimes, he thinks of Sharon naked, but he is careful not to mix this with aviculture. Joe could put parakeets in the guest bedroom.

Cages or no cages?

Cages, he thinks, but with the doors left open.

Tonya works nights at Dairy Queen, except on the weekends when Eric works. Eric is snide and seventeen, and Joe does not like him at all. But Joe is extra-polite because he is afraid that Eric will spit in his coffee. Joe is not sure if Eric has ever spit in his coffee, but the possibility tortures him. Tonya is what keeps Joe coming back. He has bought hot dogs and coffee from her several times a week for the last year. She has two long, blond pigtails, hazel eyes, and the tattoo of a dolphin on the back of her left hand. She is also seventeen, but she is not snide. And, if Joe ever does build a model railroad in his guest bedroom, he might ask Tonya if she'd care to see it. But no. That would be unromantic. One saves one's train for later in a relationship. Perhaps the parakeets, Joe thinks. Tonya hands him his hot dog and coffee through the walk-up window and says, "Have a good night."

He sits down on the wooden picnic bench alongside the building and watches the headlights of passing cars, thinking: Did she mean "Have a *good* night," as in "I'd like you to have a night that's *better* than other nights?" And, if that's what she meant, is there a veiled message there? A hidden invitation? Joe knows Tonya is subtle beyond her years. Would she come to the park and throw a Frisbee for a yellow Labrador? He cannot imagine a girl who would not appreciate colorful, free-flying parakeets. Joe takes a sip of coffee and considers.

He is on his back again, spread-eagled in the living room, and is only halfway through *A Field Guide to Aviculture*. Joe has been in a bad mood. Enough is enough. He has been expectant, waiting for her knock, for the confrontation. The fact that Sharon is content simply to watch rankles, frustrates. It has been hard to concentrate, and it bothers him that he must stand in the hallway if he wants to masturbate without her seeing through a camera. Joe goes across the street and walks around her apartment.

He scans the block from behind a hedge: no TT, no Sharon. Where could she be? He imagines her hanging on the arm of some other man—there was another man once, a garbage man from California, who she'd dated previously. He imagines her throwing a Frisbee for the garbage man's yellow Labrador. This, too, rankles, frustrates. Joe goes around to the parking lot behind her apartment and stares up at the sky.

He is not sure if he'll be able to finish the book on aviculture. He does not, presently, own any birds. And there is the added issue of the neighborhood cats electrocuting themselves on an unprotected power cable protruding from the corner of Joe's house, making it hard for him to concentrate on the text. Thinking of the spot where, only yesterday, the smoking corpse of an orange tabby lay twisted in the final throes of death, Joe asks: Why, if five cats have already died agonizing deaths, do they continue to bite the exposed cable? Do they not learn? Can there be no progress? The tabby's corpse should have been there today, when Joe went out with rubber gloves and a trash bag. Only, it was not there. The more Joe thinks about the missing cat, about the possibilities, the less sure he is, the less a missing, dead cat seems feasible: stolen by a famished rat, by a vagrant with a can of Sterno, buried by a horrified waitress on her way to work? There should be an explanation. But there is no telling why cat corpses vanish in New Orleans, why smoking, toxic rivers burst from fissures beneath the front steps, why micro-cameras appear one day in the light fixtures, or why Sharon would get involved with a garbage man from California.

Waiting in the lot behind Sharon's apartment has given Joe the opportunity to think of a plan: he will fight fire with fire. It is not a complicated plan, but it is a good one. And Joe imagines that he can almost feel a certainty about it that makes him happy. However, as with any good plan, it requires money. Hence a quick jaunt to the ATM. Hence the twenty-minute drive out to Metairie to a store called *The Cop Shop: Surveillance (audio, video, software), Tasers, Nightsticks,*

Batons — Wholesale.

Joe is no good at haggling. But when he gets there, he haggles vehemently. In the end, he buys a video surveillance kit (monitor, four micro-cams, computerized transceiver that hooks up to the VCR) for much less, he imagines, than Sharon had probably paid for hers. The sales associate is short and nervous in a sky-blue tie and too much cologne. He smiles broadly, handing Joe's change back, and decides to throw in two nightsticks for free—sleek black affairs with leather-wrapped handles. The sales associate holds one up and winks: "Take shit no more." Joe nods, silently agreeing that he is tired of taking shit.

Later, lingering in the bathtub, Joe revisits his Theory of the Sublime: There are women who are brilliant and know it, and there are men who are idiotic and don't know it. There are smart people, and there are smart donkeys and men who ride them—who are either smart or not, depending. There are beautiful women who are smart, but these you never see. There are ugly men who are stupid, who you always see. One seldom sees donkeys. Or men who are brilliant and know it. But, seeing a man who knows that he is brilliant is not unlike seeing a donkey.

The tops of his big toes are hairy. They stick out of the water. Joe questions whether a man with hairy toes can possibly be considered brilliant but rejects the question as phrenological humbuggery. "Doesn't the fact that I am sensitive to phrenological humbuggery indicate that I am intelligent? Doesn't the fact that I have a bachelor's in linguistics? That I have read Heidegger on Nietzsche and generally understood? That I am perplexed with questions of the Sublime?" Joe pictures Heidegger on Nietzsche. He pictures himself with long, furry donkey ears. Outside, the Lethe bubbles as if in accompaniment. Steam rises up from bathtub water, and Joe makes ripples with his toes.

Joe calls his psychiatrist from a payphone on Canal Street: "Trent, my ex-girlfriend has put hidden cameras in my house and sits in the apartment across the street watching me. I thought I should tell you that."

"This better not be about your payments," says Trent.

Now it is Friday. His students are shivering behind bedroom doors or suffering at work or cleaning out their attics, coughing into antique gramophones and weeping. This is how Joe imagines them. He pictures them listening to the radio and TV at full volume while their spouses scream at them. Sharon is doing whatever she does when she's not peeping on him. The waters below his house are turning the corner posts of his porch black. Cats are dying all over the world.

Stealthily, he moves across the Tulane campus, avoiding all chance contact with administrators from Tulane's Recreation and Leisure Studies Department, who have been sending him hostile memorandums, re: student complaints. To all of these, he has copied the same response: "Take it up with my psychiatrist, Trent." So far, there have been no takers.

Recreation and Leisure Studies requires him to hold an office hour for ninety minutes a week. And, every week, Joe changes the location of his "office." Today, he is holding hours in 112C of Tilden Hall, where, if he is lucky, he will soon be displaced by an intramural volleyball meeting.

Fifteen minutes have gone by and, so far, Gloria Riddel has not come to discuss her inability to perform the "Who Am I?" meditation. He cracks the door of 112C and peers up and down the hallway. He writes on the chalkboard: *Professor Joe has gone for coffee and will return shortly.*

Joe has learned that "shortly" can mean up to twenty minutes if he walks slowly to the University Center and back. He slips down the hall to 103, across an empty lecture room, and through a chipped metal door that leads to a fire escape. Joe has also learned that one is less likely to run into students or administrators on a fire escape.

In the University Center, he buys a Jumbo Java and a newspaper and takes a seat at a table where he can watch the Freshman Orientation Seminar. The new freshman girls look lovely in their tight jeans and well-planned hair. Joe will not ever teach Introduction to Meditation again, but he will miss the freshmen girls.

He looks up and notices that Gloria Riddel has tracked him here. She is perspiring heavily. "We need to talk," she says. "I got this problem—"

"With the 'Who Am I' meditation?"

"That's part of it." She arranges her bulk on the chair beside him. "So I got tight hamstrings, right? And ever since I got my gall bladder removed, when I bend, there's a popping right here." She holds his palm to her side and then slides it up so that his thumb and index finger press against the bottom of her left breast. Joe tries to pull his hand away, but Gloria holds it in place. There is a certain dampness to her floral muumuu. "What can you do to make me feel better?" she asks slowly.

Students stare at his hand as they walk by. Joe looks at the Freshman Orientation Seminar and imagines it is growing smaller and smaller.

"Well?" asks Gloria Riddel.

Buying the surveillance system has made him giddy. After office hours, he goes for a drive. Joe *tocks* the nightsticks together in their long paper bag with his shift-hand and whistles cheerily through his teeth.

He is in such good spirits he drives to Dairy Queen for a hot dog but also buys himself an ice-cream dip because he's feeling reckless. Joe sits on the picnic bench alongside the building. Tonya isn't working, but Eric is, and he shoots stink-eye at Joe through the side window. Joe taps the nightsticks in their paper bag against his thigh and stares back with maximum hostility, but the thought of spit under his relish gives him pause.

It's Saturday, and Saturday is the day of forgiveness. Joe has had a provisional change of heart. He is researching forgiveness, and Saturday is auspicious. According to his astrological almanac, it is not only the day of the new moon, it is also ruled by the sign of The Bull. And Sharon is nothing if not a Capricorn.

His Plan is ready for action, but the stars don't lie. So Joe has decided to wait. He'll give her a chance to confess. He tells himself that if she's honest about spying on him, he'll ask her out for a coffee. If she's honest about spying on him, then maybe, over coffee, he'll see whether he was wrong to break up with her. Renting an apartment to spy on one's ex must count for something: (energy)+(money)+(emotional tender)=? Joe tries to verbalize exactly why they broke up in the first place but he can't remember. And this is not something the stars can tell him.

His psychiatrist does not know about Joe's interest in astrology or that Joe has hung his own natal star-chart in the hallway—away from prying video cameras. Now, when Joe masturbates, he is compelled to stare at the degrees of Aquarius, The Water Bearer.

Joe walks across the street and knocks on Sharon's door. It's the right thing to do. No more skulking. No more intrigue. One last chance for forgiveness and redemption. The direct approach is best, thinks Joe. As a Capricorn, Sharon should appreciate that. But there is no answer. He knocks on the front door, then looks in the side window. The monitor is on, flicking from living room to bedroom to bathroom. The orthopedic swivel chair she'd bought is empty, the Joyous Wok carton desolate on her snap-together computer desk. From the window, the peanut sauce drip on the side of the carton looks dark and crusted.

Joe goes back to his front steps and sits there until sunset. Sharon's windows get dark. Spanish moss points down through the damp heat while the Lethe bubbles angrily. A rat runs back and forth on a telephone line. Somewhere, through an open window, someone is groaning, and bacon is frying. It's the evening of the day of forgiveness and, somewhere, estranged Capricorns and Aquarians are getting back together. There are 476,625 people in greater New Orleans. Of these, Joe thinks, at least 120,000 are making love tonight. Joe considers going over to Sharon's real house, but is afraid of what he might find there.

That she isn't around shows a certain faithlessness, a certain typical worthlessness. *She was always like this*, he tells himself but can't summon up a single instance in which she was. No matter. The point is simply that Sharon has bugged his house. He'll bug her back.

Across the street, her side door is unlocked, and it takes him less than five minutes to install his own mini-cameras: one in the living room, one in the bathroom, and one in the bedroom. There is no furniture other than her snap-together computer desk and orthopedic swivel chair. Joe stands off to the side of her wide living room window and peers around the edge of the curtain at his house across the street.

The cry of the Carolina parakeet was singular in its poignancy, reads Joe. He takes a bite of apple fritter and turns the page. His students are sitting cross-legged on their mats, writing answers to the final question: "How have I sought, in this class, to actualize my most inner imperatives as a human being and become more of who I already am?" The long hand of the wall clock makes an angry *thak* every minute. So far: thirty-six *thaks*, fourteen *thaks* to go. Then free at last. Then instant, golden, luminous emancipation. Joe's mood improves with every *thak*.

While the Carolina parakeet once flourished throughout the southern states, it is now extinct as the last member of its species perished in captivity in Waco, Texas, around 1918. To live out your whole life in a cage and then die in Waco, Texas, seems particularly sad. Who could have blamed the bird for taking its own life, thinks Joe. He tells himself that, in the parakeet's place, he would have succumbed long before Waco: seppuku in Amarillo, destruction in Nacogdoches. Joe wonders if Sharon's Texan parents ever kept parakeets. *Despite its natural beauty, the Carolina parakeet was often exterminated as a fruit pest, which ultimately led to its extinction, though many that were kept as pets were known to strangle themselves in the bars of their cages trying to escape.*

The class is particularly energetic today. Mr. Jenkins has filled two essay booklets and is starting a third. Gloria Riddel is scribbling furiously with a golf pencil as Byron murmurs corrections, augmentations, from the folding chair beside her. Michelle DuPont's pen makes slishing noises across the paper. And Tom Polehaus has opted to sketch a picture of how he achieved satori during the recent sale of a Model 3900 "Beast" backhoe/earth-drill. Since then, he's carried a mixture of flower petals and cloves in his suit pockets. He smiles down at the page.

When Joe's students turn in their test booklets and file out, no one says a word to him. Joe imagines that they want to put this ugliness behind them as much as he does. Michelle DuPont sniffles. Tom Polehaus winks, still smiling. Joe looks down at his book and scowls until they all leave. *Carolina parakeets were 10-13 inches long, had narrow, pointed tail feathers, emerald bodies, and yellow heads. Some had orange faces.*

The days run like wild horses over the hills, and we ride them down. When, at last, we splash through the Lethe into Elysium, we'll forget all about life on earth. In the underworld, Aeneas' father told him, before the spirits of the dead could be reincarnated, they had to drink from the Lethe to forget their happiness in paradise. *Ah*, thinks Joe, *I should re-read the fucking Aeneid. That's a book.* The smoking waters have now created a small pond around his house. On his way back from Dairy Queen, he'll have to make a long jump to get to his porch.

Going for his evening cup of coffee, Joe is perplexed by the darkness behind Dairy Queen's windows. How could they have closed early? Was that Tonya shooting by on the back of a motorcycle? Joe stands at the walk-up window and stares at his reflection in the black glass. The phonebook-yellow streetlights hiss and flutter. He imagines hundreds of giant rat eyes staring at him from the shadows of the trees.

Midriff shirts and motorcycle seats, tattoos and teen dreams, Tonya's world is closed to him completely. What did he see in Tonya anyway? If he passed her on the street, would he recognize her? Would he look twice? Joe realizes that he barely knows who she is. He can barely recall his reasons for spending so much time at Dairy Queen in the first place. Something about feeling lonely and angry, but that doesn't make any sense. He doesn't feel like that at all.

Joe looks back at Dairy Queen's dark windows, thinking how ridiculous it is to associate one's inner feelings with the local hot dog joint. And then he notices he's standing in a spreading puddle of water. The insides of his loafers are already soggy. There's something alarming about that water, the way it smokes and fumes, something toxic he'd noted previously. But, by the time Joe walks back home and sloshes up his front steps, he decides it can't be that important—a water main, a sewage line, at worst. Unlocking the front door in the dark, he hears the skitter of claws on wood.

He sits down at a bank of monitors in his living room. In one, a beautiful woman sits in front of an identical setup. It seems tragic that such a beautiful woman could look so sad. Joe watches her for a while, then walks back out on the porch. It seems that his house is sinking. He'll have to call about that water. The puddle is now starting to look more like a small pond. The porch seems lower, water licking over the top step.

Of course, Joe is slightly shocked when the beautiful woman on the monitor walks out of the apartment across the street. She takes a few tentative steps towards him. The smoking water has reached her doorstep as well and, by the time the two of them meet each other in the center of the street, a thick milky fog hangs over everything. The water is above their knees, but neither of them are bothered by that. Off to the side, a giant rat paddles through the fog. The woman smiles at him and Joe smiles back. He takes her hands in his.

The Machinery Above Us

I'd quit drinking. It had been about three months, and the anxiety attacks had stopped. I was starting to sleep nights, starting to get my sober energy back. But I was in Montana. And you don't just quit drinking in Montana. It's more complicated than that. It gets cold: you drink. The wind howls all night around your windows like it hates you and wants to come in: you drink. The used-looking girls in the bars show their tits for shots and then refuse to speak to you: you drink. The lead-gray sky is as dark as you are lonely: you drink. You ask yourself, "What am I doing here? How did I get here? And how do I get out?" And you drink.

New Year's Eve, 2001: I was *not* drinking so far and hating every minute of it, apartment sitting for a fellow graduate student, named Chris, in his place over Jay's Bar, downtown Missoula. Early evening, and I thought maybe I should go out and walk around and look at people. It was snowing, but I'd been in that apartment all day, drinking too much coffee and trying to finish a short story. There was no heater, and I'd spent the day sitting in my heavy jacket, listening to the coffee maker pop and belch, and wanting more than anything else to go downstairs and order a few pitchers of Pabst. Then I'd be able to finish the story. That's what I told myself; I knew it was alcoholic B.S. I looked out the window and, down below, I saw a mountain man smashing another mountain man's face into a parking meter. That was Montana. Happy New Year, I thought.

The mountain people came down into Missoula, mostly in summer, but you could see them all year long. They called it *the Huckleberry* because life there was a lot easier than what they were used to. They acted like bums, panhandling downtown or hitting up the college kids on Van Buren footbridge just outside the university. They were interesting and crazy and had wild stories. The downside of having them around was that they carried knives and lived off the land for a good part of every year. They didn't have that I've-been-living-on-the-street-long-enough-to-be-exhausted vibe that I remembered from the homeless in Southern California where I grew up. The mountain people were vigorous and usually vigorously drunk. When they asked you for money, they were aggressive about it.

"Gimmie dollar," an old man said to me once on the footbridge, white beard down to his waist.

"No."

"Fuck you. Gimmie dollar."

"No."

"Fuck you. I'll cut chur heart out. Gimmie dollar." That sort of thing.

So I didn't go out right away, not wanting to see blood on a parking meter that early in the evening. But, after a few minutes of my watching the mountain man with the smashed face writhe in the snow, there came a knock at the door. It was Len Stark. And, as soon as I opened the door and took a look at him, I knew what we would be doing and where the night would be going. His wife was stripping tonight, and we were going to see her. Len had never seen her work, and he'd been thinking about ambushing her for a long time, asking me whether he should, torn up inside because he'd promised her he'd never come to her place of employment. I guess he wanted to see if her stripping really was the way she told him it was or if she was a borderline hooker—what most guys hope when they walk in.

Len stood in the hallway with his hand over his nose and mouth, looking angry. "This place smells like piss."

"Just the hallway," I said.

"Well, let's go."

"You're sure about this?"

"Come on. I'm gonna puke if I smell this much longer."

"What's wrong with piss? You do it every day."

"I don't put my face in it."

I told him to give me a minute, shut off the coffee maker, and got a pack of Chris' rotten cigarettes out of the carton in the closet. I didn't usually smoke but, not drinking, I needed something. And if I had any more coffee, I'd be in the hospital.

We walked through the snow to his truck. Everything was black night or snow white, and lots of people lingered outside the bars. The bars are downtown Missoula's main attraction. Each one is slightly different with a slightly different clientele. People get falling-down drunk. People fight over women or bar stools or who has a fatter ass and crack pool cues across each other's faces. Sometimes the people act normal, but still the bar scene there is more like the Old West than anything else. And there are a lot of bars. And, every night, there are a lot of people in them. But we weren't going to just any bar. We were going to Missoula's premiere strip club, the Moulin Rouge, and we were going there for a reason other than tits, ass, and a five-dollar beer.

Of course, his wife, Winnie, didn't know we were going, and I didn't know why we had to do it now or what had piqued Len's curiosity on this particular night. But I didn't ask. Having a friend with a wife who stripped was like having a friend who had a diseased brother or a flaming-gay father. You didn't ask. You nodded and accepted and listened. When you were alone in bed at night, you thought, *Christ, don't let that happen to me*, and then you tried not to think about it anymore. It's all well and good to be hardboiled during the day, but at night it's a different story. We'd be at work, and Len would say something like, "I love her so much—she's too good for it, that job—but sometimes . . . I don't know . . . she comes home at different times." He couldn't even directly speak it. And I could have told him that she wasn't turning tricks, or that I really didn't believe she was. But then he'd have to ask me how I knew. And things would get very unpleasant.

Len's truck crunched the snow. He didn't say anything for a few blocks.

"You still not drinking?"

"Still."

"Not even a beer?"

"No. Not even a beer."

Len shook his head. "That's some Baptist bullshit like I've never heard." Len's family was Baptist, and he hated me not drinking almost as much as he hated his family.

His truck slid about six inches every time he stopped at a light. And, even though on a good day you could walk around the entire city of Missoula—including its tiny downtown and the Super Wal-Mart—in about four hours, it had been snowing heavily, and cars crept along at twenty miles an hour, speeding up in sudden, brief intervals.

"I'm writing a lot. I'm getting my work done. It's okay," I said.

Len stomped on his brakes, and we slid halfway into an intersection.

He put it in reverse. "Writers have to drink. I don't know one writer who doesn't drink."

"I'm the only writer you know."

"You're no writer," he said. The light turned green. Our wheels spun on the ice before we kicked into motion.

I'd known Len since the summer before. I'd known his wife, Winnie, a little less than that. Len and I were both twenty-two, but I was in college and he wasn't. We both worked for the City of Missoula—him because he was saving up money so Winnie wouldn't have to dance when he went off and joined the Marines in the fall, me because jobs were scarce, and it was all I could get. It was a bad job. The city called it "General Work," which meant day labor, the sort the regular city workers didn't want to do. We carried pipes in a shitfield, used saws nailed to broom handles to prune the branches of snow-covered trees, once helped demolish a thousand ancient toilets with sledgehammers at the municipal dump. We worked with the scum of the earth: mountain people, toothless people, people with so many tattoos their skin looked black, Indians banned from the rez who wouldn't say their names. Most of our co-workers smelled like booze a large part of the time. It came through their sweat like rotten citrus mixed with paint thinner. They stunk, and they didn't care. The ones who worked hardest were usually on speed.

I took out one of Chris' cigarettes. "Mind if I smoke?"

"Not in this truck you don't."

"It won't kill you," I said and lit up.

"No way would I put that shit in my body."

I did him the courtesy of blowing smoke down at the floor.

The Moulin was an expensive prospect, so Len had to stop at his brother's on the way because his brother owed him. The Sunshine Trailer Park. His brother's double-wide was covered in spider webs that had frozen into solid, crystalline patterns glittering like diamonds in the snowlight. Going in, I pushed on one, and it broke with the sound that a cheap wooden pencil makes when you snap it in half.

His brother wasn't home, but the lights and heat were on.

"Stupid motherfucker," said Len as he looked over the devastation inside. There were clothes everywhere. Dirty dishes sitting on the couch. In the sink, a stack of plates with two fat roaches sitting on top, their heads in a glob of catsup. When the cold came down, everything within the city limits died except us and the roaches. In the trailer parks, it seemed like the roaches were winning.

"Help me look for his goddamn gangster roll. He keeps it in a coffee can."

I kicked some clothes back and forth, looked in the bathroom cabinet, but it wasn't the sort of place where a can full of bills would be sitting out on a shelf.

Len was of medium build and height but had been a football star. And women in bars liked him. A few of the girls who had graduated with him at Rocky Mountain High, in Whippet, Montana, were still calling him now that they'd moved west to Missoula, finally in a city with a downtown. But Len was in love with Winnie, had known her since grade school. He'd even put up with her job, though this was the first time he wanted to go watch her work, and I could see it was making him mean. I could hear him back in the living room dumping things out, muttering invective like "Baptist piece of shit" or "Dumb bastard can't even wash his own clothes."

The bathroom mirror had white flecks on it from his brother brushing his teeth too close to the glass. I stood there and looked at myself. My hair was already going gray on the sides, and there were heavy rings under my eyes. My skin was pasty. I couldn't remember the last time I'd eaten a vegetable. I wasn't healthy, but at least I wasn't drunk. One of the problems with drinking heavily was that I'd decide to quit and then wake up days later, having missed work, having missed class, not knowing where I'd been or when I'd started up again. Sometimes I'd wake up next to someone I didn't know. Sometimes there would be things in my living room: a bike, clothes that didn't belong to me. Once I found a carbon hunting knife with dried blood on it, more than once a glistening pile of shit sitting on my carpet or in my bathtub. Vomit was a given. Naturally, I kept these things to myself. I banished them into the vault in my mind where I kept all my bad memories. But there was always leakage. A drunk carries around his bad times like a normal man carries around sin—it eats at him. He never gets away from it. It changes him. Poor Len knew none of this, and I wasn't about to lay it on him. In some ways, he was naïve. He had his own problems.

"Look at this," he said as I walked back into the living room. "Owes me seventy-five dollars and has three hundred fifty-six stashed away. Now what do you think of that?" Len had found his brother's wad. He grinned, and I could see the gold tooth on the left side of his mouth.

"Good," I said. "I hate this place. Let's go."

"At least it doesn't smell like piss."

"I'll take that trade," I said.

We went. We parked outside the Moulin Rouge. And, from the moment we stepped into the purple light, red drapes, and naked women everywhere, I knew the night was going to be difficult. If Winnie behaved as she usually did on the job, there was going to be a problem. I hadn't let myself think about it until we walked in, but then I had the fear—the feeling that I had made a grievous error being so attracted to her and coming in all the time, behind Len's back, to buy lap dances and flirt.

When we saw her, she'd just gotten off stage. Winnie was beautiful. Her hair wasn't dyed blond. It was natural, though her eyebrows were darker. She had high cheekbones, a nicely trimmed blond bush, and a well-toned body. So, of course, Winnie averaged around nine hundred a week dancing up on the catwalk for tips and at people's tables for twenty dollars a dance. She didn't have any tattoos, which made her seem just a little purer than the other girls, who'd usually had some sort of ink done at one time or another. With the kind of money she was making, Winnie only had to dance one week a month. I also think that was all Len would let her do. She'd been married to him for a year. And I'd been coming to the Moulin since I knew she worked there. On her breaks, she'd walk over and sit on my lap and bring me a club soda and shoot the shit. Because I was Len's friend, she was extra nice to me, but neither of us ever mentioned it to him. What would have been the point of that?

The Rouge was like a barn, might actually have been a barn in antiquity, with its insides painted black. More than anything else, it reminded me of the dance clubs in Tijuana I used to go to when I was sixteen: spotty track lighting and sleazy-looking drunks. You could see fashions from all the way back to the 1970s there, worn seriously. When rural Montana got away from the wife and took the truck into the city, the polyester came out. Pot-bellied ranchers would unbutton their shirts and fluff up their chest hair. And the girls were always in the process of telling them The Rules—how they expected the pie-eyed, sexed-up locals to behave while inside. "This is a gentlemen's club," they'd say. But, really, it was more like a medieval cathedral, where the sons of Montana could claim sanctuary for the night—from dried-out wives, hatred of hippies and Californians, obligatory racism, guns, and fealty to the Republican Party.

There were throngs of waitresses, who were almost, but not quite, as good looking as the strippers. *Lots* of strippers. And the obligatory gaming table that was in every public house in Montana. The liquor was always flowing. The invisible DJ was saying, "She'll be good to you if you'll be good to her" about a lackluster stripper on stage repeating the same set of moves over and over. Cigarette smoke haloed the lights. The place was packed with men and women of all shapes and sizes. We were lucky to get a table.

Len started putting away the Black Velvet as soon as we sat down—cheap Canadian whiskey that burned and smelled like acetone. He didn't take his eyes off Winnie. The club sodas were free, and I depressed the waitress right away by ordering one.

"You sure about that, sweetie?" she said, giving me the smile and wink that was designed to get the tightwads to order gin and tonics instead.

I said: "You're not a bad looking woman. But, if you ask me that question again, I'm going to complain."

"About what?" No more smiles for me.

"About nothing; you just lost your tip," I said and watched her stalk away from the table in frustration. It was the only way. Let them flirt with you, and they bring you a g&t anyway and charge you for it. What are you going to say then? That you didn't order it? That you aren't about to pay for something you don't want? The bouncers at the Moulin Rouge were a humorless bunch. Tired of human intercourse, they would only ask you once. Then you'd be tossed and beaten. They'd spit on you after they kicked you in the mouth and took your wallet. No, I practiced preventive dentistry. One club soda and my money to the girls.

I could see Len was already in pain. He'd peeled thirty dollars off his brother's roll for a lousy liter of BV, and the shot glass was traveling from bottle to table to mouth faster than I could sip my club soda. Len was unreasonable after enough hard-A. After a long night of drinking, I once ran after him chasing four frat brothers over the Higgins Street Bridge in heavy snowfall because one of the brothers had whistled at Winnie. Whistled. He'd had his folding knife with him that night, and he'd fully intended to carve them up and toss their bodies in the Clark Fork River. He didn't catch up to them, but that was only because I tackled him. So we sat there and watched his wife take care of business, giving personal dances and making her husband get whiter and straighter by the minute in his plush chair. She hadn't seen us yet. I wasn't sure what would happen when she did. But I was sure that it would be nasty and upsetting. And I could see myself running for dear life over Higgins Street Bridge before the end of the night.

An interesting thing to note about Missoula—and I suspect this is true with most small towns—is that wherever you go, you're bound to recognize someone. Another interesting thing to note is that the story in which the boyfriend/husband of the stripper goes to watch her strip and winds up wrecking the joint is universal. It's in the script, as my father used to say when he'd predict the actions of one of our neighbors or the scores of a ballgame. Unfortunately, this one was an open-ended script, one in which the outcome of the story is not as easy to foresee. To wit: I could sense the machinery of the night clicking into place above us. The evil was building in Len to the point where he was going to have to be restrained sooner or later—sooner if Winnie started to get hot and heavy with someone he didn't like, later for sure. But things hadn't progressed to the point at which me ducking out seemed inevitable. Besides, Gregory the Dwarf had sat down at our table, and I didn't want to be impolite.

"What's wrong with Halloween?" said Gregory.

I just smiled and shrugged. Gregory was drinking bourbon and had lost any sense of tact. Whenever we saw him in the bars, he referred to Len as Halloween. He had names for everybody—mostly for the more unattractive women. One of them, who always wore a bright orange jacket, was The Great Pumpkin. Another he called Reptilicus, after a monster in an old 1970s horror movie. Another was Leviathan. Golgotha. Behemoth. The Beast. And Gregory really was a dwarf. He drank himself sick every night and had broken his arms more than once falling off barstools. He had to be at least fifty, but who could tell? The only thing certain was that Gregory was a mean sonofabitch and didn't like anyone. I knew he was going to start hassling us. If he learned the reason we were there, that would be the end.

I thought: jail, assault, probation, fines, community service. I thought: back door, through the snow, bar across the street, pay phone, taxi, nice warm bath in Chris' rusted claw foot tub.

"What is this? A funeral? We've got naked bitches up everywhere, and you two look about as dead as dead. What do you say, Halloween?"

"Don't try me, Gregory," said Len, his eyes still on his wife. "You're trying me. And I'll hit a dwarf."

"You'll hit shit"—which made no sense, but Gregory frowned and nodded after he said it as if that settled things.

I put my arm around his little shoulders. "Look, man, let me buy you a drink." But that was wrong.

He stood up and slammed his empty rocks glass down on the table, which was chest high on him. "Don't you fuckin' look at me. Don't you fuckin' condescend to me."

He wobbled a bit, looked around, and pulled out his pecker. Before he could piss on me, a bouncer had wrapped his hand around Gregory's throat.

"You're done, little man," said the bouncer, who was large compared to anyone, but who looked like a mountain next to Gregory.

Gregory pissed on his leg, and the bouncer backhanded him hard across the mouth—more embarrassed that the other bouncers were laughing at him than angry at Gregory—and carried him toward the door.

Len's belligerence might not have surfaced, and things might not have been so bad, might have ended there—it's not inconceivable—if Corey Martlet hadn't come in, talking loud. Corey, with his pig-sausage fingers, gut, and big mouth, was the sort of guy who went to the Moulin Rouge and tipped cheap, put his hands where his hands weren't supposed to go, and made fun of the girls after he left. A real shit-heel.

It went like this: the strippers would take you to a dark corner and do their dances in front of you. They wouldn't make illegal contact, but they could grind on you and rub themselves up against you while you sat there. Usually everything was professional and polite. They'd do their thing, and you'd pay them and tip them a little extra, and they'd smile and thank you. You'd thank them and then go away feeling a little better than you did before. That was the point. But some people went in there, men and sometimes women, with a different agenda. They bought personal dances because they wanted to see a girl do something for them, preferably something degrading—the more degrading the better. And in their minds, stripping was dirty. They didn't get off by looking at a beautiful body; they got off on the power trip that came from whispering filthy things to the girl or touching her privates while she danced. Corey Martlet was one of those people. He was also our supervisor at work.

He held up a hundred for five dances, all five from Winnie—which meant the duration of five songs—while the main girl was pole dancing on the catwalk. Winnie didn't have a choice. We'd seen it coming, and Len was standing up before she even got Corey across the room. I stopped him. I said: "Come on, Len, you knew this could happen." But here was Corey Martlet getting grinded on by Len's wife. And Corey knew it. He'd seen us when he came in, and he was enjoying the hell out of it.

There were times at work when I thought he wanted to kill us. He'd shift his fat ass on that little padded stool behind his desk and smile when we'd come in for an assignment, grinning because there was some septic problem he'd found for us to fix or a filthy elevator shaft full of football-sized rats he could send us into. Why was he like this? I'm not certain. I like to think he was just inherently lousy, but I'm sure it had to do with the fact that Len had a pretty wife and I was a graduate student and neither of us planned to stay in that job.

From where we were sitting, we had to look across the catwalk, but we could see everything, even though the Moulin Rouge was dark. Winnie had a nice tan, a perfect ass, and her hair was long. She let it hang down over Corey Martlet's face while she grinded, then turned around and lay back against him. She had to keep slapping his hand away from her crotch. And, once, she stood up and admonished him for something (we couldn't hear) before getting back to work.

I thought about all the times I'd bought dances from Winnie and how, breaking the house rules, she'd kissed me when no one could see. I thought about the night I drove her home, how we'd made out in my car with Len asleep ten feet away. Once or twice, she'd suggested we get together and fuck whatever attraction we had out of us so we could stay friends and things wouldn't be weird. But the logic of that escaped me. She'd insisted it wouldn't mean anything, though I knew it would. And I wondered how many "friends" she really had. These were things I had to bury deep down when I was around Len because I was afraid they'd show when the three of us were out together or at an odd, unguarded moment when Len was talking about her.

Regardless, I should have read the script more carefully. I should have taken Len out right then, but I was getting wrapped up in the whole thing—watching Winnie's face, the way she moved, her back. So when Len sprang up, I was too slow. He ran around to the other side of the club, pulled her off, and yanked Corey out of his seat. The bouncers were fast. They knew what to do, and Len didn't. They put him in a hold, almost broke his arm half-carrying him out the door.

The front steps of the Rouge were black cement rounded like a dais, and they had a red felt carpet staple-gunned to them, suggesting that just a little bit of Hollywood had hunkered down in Missoula and folded its wings. Len sailed over these steps and landed face first in the snow, which was pink from the lights on the outside of the building. I ran to help him up.

Corey stood behind a bouncer, jabbing a sausage-finger at the air. His face was red. "Screw you, Stark, screw YOU, you dumb fucking redneck. Go back to your fucking trailer." Corey was alternately smiling and frowning like he'd been waiting for this all his life and, now that it was happening, he didn't know whether to be angry or pleased.

I tried to hold Len back, but we slipped in the snow and both fell, him on top of me. Struggling back to his feet, he accidentally hit me in the eye with his elbow, which hurt and sent me back to the ground. I remember seeing one of the bouncers chuckle at this. On my knees in the snow, I wondered if now would be the time to split, but I couldn't light out for home as I knew I'd have to face Len later. Two more bouncers had come out on the steps to flank the first two, and now they all had aluminum softball bats.

Len was screaming at Corey to take off his diaper and come down into the snow, calling him a fat fuck. Fists clenched, red flannel shirt, jeans, and work boots: Len would have been perfect for an old Soviet propaganda poster: Proletarian Justice! It was interesting that I was having this thought in the middle of this situation. It was even more interesting that not once did either of them mention Winnie. And I wondered how much of this was simply due to the fact that Corey sent us out on the worst assignments and then gloated about it later, when we came back in the truck heavy-hearted, covered in mud or shit.

One last time, I tried to hold Len back. I did this, not on principle, but because I didn't want to see him crippled—especially not in front of his wife, who was peeking around the edge of the door. But Len was past reason. Whiskey and jealousy and straight-up Montana stupidity had conspired to make him Superman. And what were four bat-carrying bouncers to Superman? He rushed the steps. The first two bouncers wound up and took out his knees as if they'd choreographed this. Synchronized Beating. The next two kicked him in the ribs. When he tried to get up, the pommel of a bat came down on his face. The beating went on for a little while longer, until the bouncers had gotten it out of their systems.

One of them walked back inside to call an ambulance. The other three looked at me. I was standing there, I imagine, with a very sad expression on my face. Corey was still up on the steps, looking like he needed a cigarette, like this was the most action he'd ever seen for a hundred dollars, and he was fully satisfied. There was an oval of bloodstained snow underneath Len. When I walked towards him, one of the bouncers made a threatening gesture at me with his bat, and I held my hands up in the international sign language for Please Don't Hurt Me.

"Go," said the bouncer.

So I turned and walked. I stared at the snow all the way home. I remember looking at black windows in ancient brick office buildings. When the story is a universal one, and the machinery has started to turn above you, there's not a whole lot you can do—especially when you live in Montana, it's been snowing hard all night, and some crazy girl sitting in the bed of a passing truck screams "Happy Fucking New Year!" while your buddy's en route to the hospital. I remember an empty pint bottle of Wild Turkey sticking out of the snow, how moonlight got caught in its curves and made them glow green.

Mansions for the Crows

Ayllene Heisen stood at the edge of the quay, her white dress rippling in the breeze, and pointed at Captain Paul as he walked down the gangway.

"*You* have a parcel for *me*," she said, sounding like she was in charge of the quay, the mail ship, and all of the islanders as well. Half of them were occupied with unloading wooden crates, bundles of lumber tied with thin metal stripping, and the giant burlap bags marked POSTAL. The rest of them looked down at us from the rails and rigging of the mail ship.

They're scrutinizing us, I thought, but I really had no idea what they were thinking. In all the summers we'd come to Saint Dîme, I had perhaps spoken with the native islanders less than ten times. They knew who we were, and where we'd come from, and they usually avoided us. There weren't many whites to be found, in those days, who weren't staying in West Ballou, the small town that had been purchased by the DGI Corporation to house its vacation time shares.

Captain Paul was an islander. There was no doubt about that, despite the fact that his French and English were both without Caribbean accent. He switched indiscriminately between the two: "*Puisque Marc avait mal au dos, il ne pouvait pas marcher vite.* And so we are late again with the post," he sighed, "and the price is double." His brother, Marc, stood behind him, shrugging and smiling sheepishly, showing off his gold front teeth. Captain Paul's forearms bulged when he crossed them, and his dreadlocks curved up slightly at the ends as if whatever he'd used to stiffen them had curdled in the heat.

I began to study the tops of my shoes, looking up only to glance at Neils Irish, who was interested in something far out over the bay. Ayllene crossed her own arms. "Do you really think, captain, do you really think that's professional?" She could be insufferable. She was only at "Self-Righteous" but, soon, I knew, she'd be Inconsolably Angry then potently Insufferable. It was the way she worked. And I loved her (yes: quietly, painfully) in spite of it, maybe even because of it. Her naturally red hair had a golden tint and shined in the sun.

Captain Paul chuckled, jovial with just a pinch of derision underneath his dimples. He looked at us and waited, his arms bulging dangerously, while his men cleaned their nails with curved daggers and stared.

On all of the Leeward Islands, as far as I could tell, it was customary to pay for one's mail. The captain could expect at least fifty dollars, American, for a medium-sized package, perhaps more if he'd gone through any extra trouble—as in his brother's bad back, one more nautical mile off his usual course, an extra ten minutes docked at Cavis, et cetera. So he waited. And Neils and I waited. And the growing crowd of impatient islanders here for their mail waited—for Ayllene.

"Will we do business?" he said, continuing to smile, adding, *"Tu n'as pas d'amis ici"* when Ayllene made no response. The crowd behind us quieted. Captain Paul had noted a very simple fact: we had no friends here. Who would help us or care if we were chopped to pieces and fed to the sharks in the bay? I didn't want to be chopped to pieces and fed to the sharks in the bay.

Ayllene had crossed her own arms now, and I began to worry in earnest. We looked like imbeciles—Neils with his hands clasped before him as if he were in church, me in my Bermuda khakis and Hawaiian shirt, and Ayllene forgetting that she was not at home and that Captain Paul was not her housekeeper.

Marc gestured at the air and coughed lightly a few times, breaking out into another grin: *"Rien n'est important quand on est malade."* And the captain began to laugh along with a few of his men.

Ayllene was still angry. I could sense an outburst bubbling inside her. So I took a hundred dollar bill out of my wallet and handed it to the captain, who slipped it into his pocket without ever looking away from Ayllene. I accepted the package from one of the sailors, but by the time I turned around, she was already heading back along the trail lined with white boulders all the way up the cliffs. She was fuming, but it wouldn't last. Today, we would watch the airships from the clearing above West Ballou. I knew that would cheer her up.

I was right. Soon she was talking nonstop and gesturing as she always did, despite the fact that the three of us had clearly reached an impasse, as Ayllene walked ahead that afternoon, happily insisting once again to us and the world that she was pregnant, though, unfortunately, and as I pointed out whenever this particular brand of make-believe cropped up, the Immaculate Conception stopped being an option for virgins about two thousand years ago.

There was no longer any ground for us to cover, in our triangular friendship, that had not already been covered again and again as the summer wore itself out over West Ballou. Still, we were going to see the airships, and I think it's safe to say that we were driven on towards the grassy meadow above the town—not by a desire for new stimulation but from the sheer determination not to give in to ennui. Our situation had everything to do with being overstimulated, pampered white teenagers in a predominantly black island community. Yes, we were often horrible. We were shameless. What little there was to do, we'd already done a hundred times, treating everyone and everything with the utmost contempt.

We were difficult. We teetered on the edge of total war with ourselves and the island. We'd taunt each other, well aware of each other's weaknesses: Neils' fear of hummingbirds and the large Caribbean spiders that preyed on them; Ayllene's need—then and always—to plan the next fifty years of her life as mother-ballerina, mother-lawyer, mother-neurosurgeon, the greatest mother who'd ever lived; and my loneliness, even among these friends I'd known my whole life, on evenings when I'd disappear down to the quay below West Ballou and stare at the water—which was all Ayllene and Neils needed to call, *Max, oh Max, why so down in the dumps? Oh, tell us what could be wrong* in the most patronizing voices possible.

We'd sit, drinking mint tea and *citronades* with gin on the terrace of the Café Dubonnet until we could barely walk, and I feared we'd get approached by The Jacques, the town idiot. He'd stand across the street, staring at us through layers of grime and filth-stained whites, occasionally looking down to address the glistening fruit beetles he kept trapped in his pockets.

We'd strip to our underwear, diving into the Great Salt Pond near the tip of Dragon's Head until our eyes became red and swollen from the salt. And the friendship ring I'd given to Ayllene turned an embarrassing ochre from the water, though the street vendor had promised me it was half-weight sterling.

We'd build things—mansions of cards, the giant pagoda of crisp-breads that we'd sprayed golden-yellow with Oil of Vienna from the cans we'd found in a basement of one of the time shares. The pagoda became a yellow marvel: fifteen tiers of crisp-breads reaching up from the verandah—a grand, Chinese Babylon, stinking of all-purpose machine oil, and covered with cockroaches within thirty minutes of the spraying—which brought the local crows swooping down in a mad sight.

And, mostly, we read. We read in Saint Dîme perhaps even more furiously than we normally did. Back home, in the small park in the middle of Deutsche Gesellschaft Information's arcology, we'd sip tea after school and discuss what books we were reading, quietly enjoying each other's company. Everything in the universe would be in its proper place. The temperature would be perfect. DGI employees and their families would be sitting at comfortable distances from each other. And a quiet, relaxing murmur would mingle with the sweet smell of freshly cut grass. The arcology was just a few miles outside Baton Rouge, but the infamous Louisiana humidity never came down through the geodesic extoframe that covered the arcology like a giant carapace. There, the sun was always diffuse and gentle.

West Ballou was an altogether different environment: the air was breezy and laced with salt that burned the skin when the wind blew too hard. We'd grown sun-blistered and sore after our first week, just like all the other times we'd come. So, being miserable, as we always were when we'd have to live for three weeks in the eggshell-pink time shares overlooking the ocean, we'd plow through whatever books we could find, stacked and moldering, that had been left in the time shares over the years.

We were arcology kids, privileged children of the corporate middle class. And, though we knew everything, we'd done nothing—nothing real, at any rate. Whatever frame of reference we had came from books or the incessant four hundred and sixty channels of premium cable bandwidth streaming into our living rooms. There was no experimentation with controlled substances; there were no parties—except very quiet get-togethers on the grass in Arcology Center or in Woodglen Shopping Mall—quaint, heavily surveiled areas for the rare few with enough time and energy on their hands to loiter.

The first arcologies, formed by IBM and Sirius Microsystems, were work-intensive, with the families of engineers, management, and labor all living within blocks of each other—whole cities devoted to corporate productivity. Unfortunately, the early ones had floundered in suicides, divorces, alcoholism, and the occasional deserter being run down and arrested for violation of the terms of employment (which has been, for years, a matter of contractual fraud). Now suicides were down by 70 percent, though divorces and alcoholism were still ongoing problems. Arcologies were better, smarter, and we were told that DGI's was the most successful ever. We took psych evals once a month, and there were lots of grassy areas.

We lived in Shadow Brook, the management neighborhood at the south end of the complex, and everyone agreed it was very nice. There were five different models of houses, which all came with balustrades and balconies, sunrooms with remote-powered skylights, and swimming pools that glistened bright turquoise in the soft filtered sun. There were some who never saw a reason to buy into the time share beach houses that DGI maintained on Saint Dîme and Saint Croix. Everything necessary for a happy life had been provided in the arcology.

When we got up to the time shares, we saw trouble over at the main entrance. The islanders avoided us as a rule, but the lepers were an exception. And today, they were out en masse. There were at least fifteen of them crowding at the yellow mechanized barricade attached to the guardhouse. West Ballou had a high stone wall around it, topped with black wrought-iron spikes, except where the road curved up from Bosquet or the time shares faced out, over the cliffs, toward the ocean. There was no way to approach from the cliff unless you were on the quay trail—supplemented, in places, by a small wooden stair or steps cut directly into the earth.

As we entered the town, we joined the crowd in the middle of the road, watching the lepers tap on the glass of the guardhouse, where a DGI security officer stood nervously shaking his head and waving his hands. The barricade was really no obstacle, even to the lepers in their cowls and rags. It was the sight of the revolver strapped high on the guard's chest that held them back.

"Every summer, one of them tries to slip by to beg while the others are making a ruckus," said Dr. Forrest, one of DGI's senior electrical engineers. We always listened to what he had to say, not only because he'd been coming to West Ballou for as long as we could remember but also because, in that time, he'd learned a lot of things we hadn't. Important things, like how to get a ride in an airship, when you could get free lobsters in Bosquet, and when it was safe to dive off the cliffs and not get sucked into the dangerous funnel made by waves collapsing in on themselves at the bottom.

My mother was there, in her white sun visor, flirting with Dr. Forrest, as she always did. She had a basket of blood-red geraniums hooked over her forearm. She'd lean towards the squat little man like a reed bending over a boulder, and blush, whispering something in his ear that made him chuckle and jounce. Even as young as I was, I knew what my mother was about. She acted like that every summer. My father was oblivious. He and Toby Irish looked the same—both smoking cigars in their white knit polos and velcroed culottes. They stood forward, lost in conversation under the eaves of the whitewashed restaurant that chefs from the arcology opened every night. Whenever my father and Neils' father were sobering up, they smoked cigars that came in white metal tubes. And, for weeks, even after several launderings, all our vacation clothes would smell like those cigars.

I felt Ayllene's fingertips on the back of my neck. "I want to go," she whispered.

Four more guards, armed with assault rifles and riot armor, stood abreast between us and the lepers at the barricade.

"Fifty says one gets through," called Jim Zane, the new head of personnel. He had black hair slicked straight back, and he never appeared without khakis and a pressed button-down. He was sweating heavily in the strong Caribbean sun. It was the first time I had seen him without a tie. "Come on, guys," he laughed. But my father just waved his hand without turning, immersed as he was in a conversation with Dr. Irish.

"I don't want to see this," said Ayllene, louder now.

And Neils: "Please, Max, this'll just bring us down."

The guard had sunk below the windows of the guardhouse, and some of the lepers were hobbling away as fast as they could. But a few—impossible to tell whether they were new or not as I'm sure their rags were inherited—stood dumbly gripping the yellow barricade or still tapping on the guardhouse glass. Three of the guards in the street aimed their assault rifles. The fourth spoke through a megaphone: *You are trespassing on privately owned property. Please step back one hundred feet from the barricade.*

Jim Zane swore quietly to himself and crossed his arms, shifting his weight nervously back and forth. I watched him steal quick, resentful glances at my father and Toby Irish, who sent plumes of smoke over the dirt street and gestured with their cigars.

This is your final warning. Move back one hundred feet from the barricade or we will use force.

"Please, Max," said Ayllene, in the desperate, throaty whisper that would have moved me in any other circumstances.

"No, Al," I said. I set her box down and wouldn't look at her. I'd heard about this but had never actually seen it happen. I knew Ayllene had, at least. My parents usually made sure I was nowhere around when the lepers came. I could remember seeing them once before, as my mother led us down the quay trail to take pictures of gulls that glided over the calm water down and away from the cliffs, where the quay floated on hollow shipways.

The guard who'd been speaking picked up his own rifle, and there was a clacking sound, the sound of industrial presses or someone running thick strips of plastic along the pickets of a fence. Thick, gauzy smoke whorled around the shoulders of the guards.

My mother turned her face away and leaned on Dr. Forrest's round shoulder for support. "Oh my god, those poor people," she said, shading her mouth with the back of her hand, as if it were the first time she'd seen this, though I knew it wasn't. This allowed Dr. Forrest to pat her on the small of the back and chuckle some more, "Rubber bullets," he said, "rubber bullets is all."

Not a leper was standing.

Neils came up beside me, hands in the pockets of his twill slacks, and furrowed his brow in the way he only did when he was angry. "Max? Can we go now?"

I watched Jim Zane give my father and Toby Irish a dark look before stalking away, his arms still crossed. And there was my mother, holding up her basket of geraniums to Dr. Forrest, who bent down to look at them closely. His thick round glasses slipped back a little when he wrinkled his nose and held a geranium up for scrutiny as if it were a glass of fine wine.

Ayllene tugged on the back of my Hawaiian shirt, but I wouldn't budge. I wanted to wait until the lepers got up and left, just as we waited in church every Sunday for the minister to walk down the center aisle. There was a certain solemnity to it.

As soon as the last leper moved, the guards would use flame units to scorch the earth. Dr. Forrest had told us they really didn't need to, but someone had once asked that they do it, and now it was standard procedure. They were already strapping on the small white backpacks shaped like turtle shells, with tubes that ran to long nozzles.

My father and Neils' father stopped in front of us.

"Having a good time?" asked my father with a wry expression, grinding the butt of his cigar into the dirt. Dr. Irish had the same look, and neither of their expressions changed when Neils replied, "Yes, sir."

"Good," said Dr. Irish. "Neils, zip your fly."

Neils gasped and looked down, blushing a deep red. Off at the barricade, there was a thick hissing as bulbous clouds of fire leapt and vanished in the air.

We'd gone to see the airships enough times to get bored with them, then faintly interested, then extremely curious in the way of those desperate to rediscover old excitements. Swimming in the abandoned iron cistern on the outskirts of West Ballou, we'd discuss which of the airship pilots had the best chances. Ayllene favored Nan Tessier because she said he was *venerable* and still handsome. Neils would always argue Achad the Arabian or Piet Morneau, though neither of them had won a race in the last thirty years. Most of the pilots had been flying for about that long—all of them old mail pilots who could remember the days when pirates had effectively eliminated delivery by ship, and small zeppelins carried everything from letters to machine parts to the huge bricks of gutta-percha that the islanders carved for awnings and tires.

We'd splash in the dark water of the cistern after sundown, talking about airships and books. The iron of the cistern was so old that it was rusted black, making the small circle of evening sky, shining through the cistern's open hatch, the only piece of color in a pitch universe. And I always argued that Ladislaw Vrtel would win because he actually *did* have a good record of wins, and he was a Czech, a foreigner, like us. And, like us, I imagined he might someday do something unpredictable, remarkable, something utterly beyond himself.

I told myself we would be this way: Neils would grow up and be mature and put his mother's suicide behind him. Ayllene would see that I was the one she'd been waiting for all along. And I? I would move to Paris and then to Marrakech, where I would start a café in which people could smoke heavily and listen to old Édith Piaf forty-fives. And they'd feel like they should let me know when they were going out of town, so I wouldn't be hurt when they came back saying, *Max, Max, I was in the Yukon, and I met the most interesting old hunter* or *There it is, John Dillinger's favorite Tommy gun — it'll be sold at Tiffany's next month, but I just thought I'd bring it by and* . . . I told myself all of it could happen. Maybe if Vrtel won, I thought. Maybe then.

I was carrying the box, which meant I had to step cautiously, because Ayllene had reminded me no less than five separate times on the long walk up from the quay, that it contained every last bit of valuable matériel we could honestly hope for in our daily war on boredom. In short, it held the Heisen family memorabilia—all that was left when her grandfather, Emiel Heisen, in a fit of florid schizophrenia, burned everything he owned in the hold of his square-rigger, *Das Futhark,* including the ship itself. It went down off Thisted, in the North Sea, and one of few things the rescuers salvaged was a small slatboard crate containing several hermetically sealed plastic containers with "Ayllene Heisen" written on them in Marks-A-Lot. Now the box had arrived and, because her family apparently had no interest in the things Emiel Heisen may have intended for his granddaughter, we were the only ones there when the mail ship put in.

We had not yet opened it, wanting to extract every last drop of excitement possible. In our extreme boredom, we pretended that the box contained a fortune and that Ayllene would never have to work in her life, though she was already eighteen and had thus far managed to avoid the all the character-building volunteer jobs around the arcology, into which Neils and I had been forced by our respective families. All our parents belonged to the same benevolent societies, worked in the same R&D division, and were accustomed to taking vacations together—which meant I was tormented by Ayllene's beauty and Neils' naïveté in Saint Dîme every summer.

One more month, and I knew Ayllene would depart for Yale, where I'd lose her forever into its great maw. There, she'd be changed permanently, and I would be left saddled with Neils Irish for yet another summer, alone this time, before I'd be old enough to follow. Just once, before the end of the summer, I wanted to sit beside Ayllene in the grassy meadow above West Ballou—without Neils Irish—and watch the airships race slowly over Bosquet and South Cathedral's Bay.

We all knew it was unlikely that Ayllene was ever going to have to work no matter what she did, imaginary pregnancy or no, seeing that members of her family were on the supreme court of Louisiana and she was filthy rich. And though we were on Saint Dîme, halfway around the world, and though Neils Irish's family and mine were also fairly well-fixed, I was painfully aware that the comfort of my late childhood was rapidly ticking down. Having reached sixteen-and-a-half, I felt that my junior year at the arcology's academy had produced in me a deep world-weariness.

And Neils Irish, despite his usual upbeat disposition, was really no different. He was the only son of Toby Irish, the chemical engineer famous for inventing an organic circuitry capable of imitating the functions of the human neocortex. And Toby Irish spared his son nothing: micropore-synthesized drop jacket, pairs of Diesel jeans, sweaters from Dolce Italia Internationale, a new Daimler SLK230 Kompressor that Neils never drove because no one drove in the arcology. There was no need as one could traverse the entire community, from the production-storage facilities in the north, to the eastern education-recreation complex, to the neighborhoods in the south, and up through the shopping-administrative center along the western arc of the extoframe. Cars were an affectation. If you owned a nice one, you let it sit in your driveway because there were no real roads, and few people went on non-company trips. Most driveways were empty, pristine concrete, as many of our parents' colleagues planned to stay even after they retired.

Neils and I often walked the arcology after dark. And it was on one of these walks that he confided to me his hatred for his father—that he suspected his father of resynthesizing some of the Veronal tablets his mother took to get to sleep at night, upping the potency a hundredfold.

"She'd never kill herself," he'd said, "not like that," staring at the area lights reflected in the mirrored windows of Storage Complex D. We'd thrown small pastel-colored rocks at the windows, watching the glass ripple. We knew the windows would never break. They were too well-engineered.

The pills she'd taken had been far beyond the normal potency. And the official story was that she'd had a friend on the outside—an old lover from before Neils' parents met and moved to DGI. Toby Irish claimed that she'd received and sent letters and that she had often talked on the phone with her phantom lover late into the night. He was the one who supposedly sent the pills. But there was no proof. Neils' mother had burned a lot of things the day before she died. The investigators had found the ashes in a flowerpot beside their pool.

I'd always wondered if his mother's death was what caused Neils to be so soft, so passive. He hadn't always been that way. He was just as intelligent as Ayllene and me, but his grades were up and down. He enjoyed calculus but hated chemistry, French, history, and memorization of any sort. He preferred to lie on the grass reading J.G. Ballard novels until security would come over and ask him to sit on a bench, as lying down by yourself in public was unattractive and discouraged.

I tried not to look at anyone in particular when we reached the meadow. But Ayllene was much better at blocking people out than me. She hardly paid attention to either of us and pretended she was talking to herself, as we stood on the huge white rocks splintered throughout the meadow. Far off in the valley beside the city of Bosquet, the white airships were floating hundreds of feet off the ground, pulling up guidelines and dropping ballast.

"Hypatia. Hypatia's a good name, an artistic name," Ayllene said, hugging herself in the breeze.

Hypatia might have been artistic, but the highest point on Saint Dîme was Mt. Miatura. And, being the name of a mountain 1156 meters high, it was, I felt, a much more interesting and progressive name for a girl who didn't exist. Miatura. Miatura Heisen had a nice ring. Everyone would love it. She would love it. We'd call her Mia for short. Turie as a term of endearment. Of course, there was the question of the father, given the fact that none of us had ever had carnal relations in our lives.

"Hypatia's nice," said Neils, wiping his hand on his crepe sweater vest.

We stood in the long grass and watched Jean Arnot's small zeppelin begin to drift forward and up, the bright red "A" on its side very striking against the white chassis. Neils handed me his digital telescope and, through its powerful imaging system, I could see Arnot gesturing violently at a map, his co-pilot, Tommy Lyon, looking very concerned. The propellers on the back of the gondola began to spin.

Ayllene opened her backpack, taking out dark pears, a round shepherd's bread, and the squat bottle of anisette she'd stolen from the stockpile of liqueurs her mother had begun as soon as we all arrived on the island. At *le commissaire* in Bosquet, one could find almost any drink. And it seemed to me that all the liquor in the world was there—bottles of every conceivable color, the labels of which were often in languages I'd never heard spoken—bare-chested women with laughing mouths open to receive bunches of grapes, silver steppe wolves in mid-spring, yellow volcanoes erupting behind Japanese characters.

Ayllene set the bottle of anisette in the grass. The hard sunlight trapped inside made its beveled edges glow. Its label showed a bushy anise plant with a bright orange caterpillar climbing one of its stems.

"Hypatia might be it," said Ayllene, "or Ivy."

I put her grandfather's box beside the anisette. "Should we open it?"

"Let's wait," said Neils, nervously sucking air past his teeth. "The race is just starting."

Bosquet is on the Caribbean side of Saint Dîme. The airships had just enough fuel to travel down, over South Cathedral's Bay, through the narrows that separate Saint Dîme from the island of Cavis, and then up the North Atlantic side, turning west over the island at Upper Sauterelle and landing, once again, at Bosquet. It wasn't a fast race, but few things were fast on Saint Dîme—perhaps the gulls or the nameless blue-green water snakes said to infest the bay, though we had never seen any.

Ayllene stretched her arms so high that her T-shirt rode up the small of her back, and I saw the line where bikini sunburn was becoming bikini tan. "I think I might take a nap. The sun's so warm," she said, yawning and stretching out in the grass.

"But the race just started." Neils looked forlorn like a puppy shooed out of the kitchen.

She laced her hands behind her head and didn't answer.

"Come on, Neils," I said, but he just stared at Ayllene with his hands in his pockets, loudly sucking his teeth. "Come on, we'll go have a smoke."

We walked to the other side of the meadow, and I took out the blue-white box of Gitanes I'd stolen a few nights before, when my mother and father had gotten too drunk.

Neils coughed but only smoked more fiercely.

The meadow was high and open, and we could see most of the western side of the island. Far behind us, near the northern tip of Saint Dîme, Mount Miatura's peak presided over everything. It was good to smoke. The wind was heavy and made the embers of our cigarettes pulse.

"Did you know flying in an airship is actually very hazardous?"

"Don't worry about Ayllene," I said. "She's just upset because I made us watch the lepers."

"Hydrogen gas isn't used anymore in dirigibles."

"It's my fault if anything, Neils. She'll get over it."

He ground his cigarette into the grass and looked at me for a long moment. "In Germany, they're experimenting with low-weight hydrocarbon fuels. They could take those big Daimler engines out of the airships."

"Then we'd see a race."

"Yeah," he said, wistfully watching the last airship lift-off—Achad the Arabian's—with the long, discolored patch near its rudders. "If they just used helium, it would be safer. It's a safer lifting gas."

Across the meadow, only a small swatch of Ayllene's T-shirt was visible in the waving grass. I looked back at her and then crossed my arms against the wind, staring down with Neils at whitecaps forming on the bay.

"Windy today. Not a good day for airships."

"My dad said crows ate the body of a leper once. Said one time a leper actually made it in at night and fell over. And, in the morning, they found his half-eaten body in the street. You think that's true, Max?"

"I don't know," I said. "He's your dad."

"He's going crazy," said Neils, slowly, watching the whitecaps flatten and elongate into waves that spat and sparked against the cliff like electricity. "He talks to my mom at night."

The airships had become a train of floating pearls, far off over Dragon's Head. Even with the telescope, it was hard to tell who was ahead.

"Vrtel is going to win this time. I can feel it." I squinted into the telescope, upping the magnification to x500.

"What's going to happen next year, Max? What'll become of us? Ayllene's going, I mean, and then you . . ." He frowned and tensed his brow like he could see the future reflected in the bay if he only concentrated.

"Neils, come on, Vrtel has a chance. I'm telling you. He's going to do it."

"I don't think the lepers come to beg like everybody claims," Neils said. "I think they come because they're lonely."

Down on the quay, the smokestack of Captain Paul's

mail ship sent up a transparent black fume as gulls shot over the water like white arrowheads.

"Hey. Come on," shouted Ayllene, holding up the box. "I could give birth any minute. We've got to open this."

Neils and I looked at each other. "Vrtel might have a chance," he said.

We walked back across the meadow. I was glad we'd waited to open the box. We'd speculated about its contents for so long that now, I had to admit, it could contain anything.

Gravity

Oh, the puppy. Everyone wept for the puppy. Tears rolled down my wife's cheeks as she cried through the night. Little Jessica next door wouldn't say hello and took a week off from school. Jessica's mother stopped coming outside and stopped speaking to me altogether. The puppy. Little fluffy puppy that didn't have a name. Big brown eyes. Pink tongue. It was so cute. Someone decapitated it with a shovel. After that, its cuteness declined. It's useless to add, when our neighbor was hit on his bicycle last year and sent at high velocity through the trunk of the tree across the street, his cuteness also declined. The man was forty-five, a mechanic with three DUIs and a failed marriage, who couldn't look you in the eye. When it happened, my wife, Cheryl, said: "Too bad he's dead," and walked in the other room.

Yes, I thought, too bad. Too bad was what it was.

I thought the same thing watching Cheryl get nailed by Gary, our attorney, on a day I was supposed to be out looking for work. I stood outside our open bedroom window, briefcase in hand, my tie, my overcoat, watching Gary give it to her from behind. The sound of his body slapping against my wife's ass made me a bit upset. I was somewhere in the vicinity of "too bad," or maybe something a little stronger, when I drank half a bottle that night and rolled Cheryl's Accord into a ditch. Given enough time, all things wind up in a ditch by the side of the road. Our airborne neighbor should have known that.

Maybe not the puppy. Certainly Gary. And my wife.

Mister .38-caliber knew it. Every time I looked into his dark mouth, he repeated it to me. Ditches: the end of all things with broken windshield and sincerest regrets. I hope you remembered your seat belt. If not, well, that's too bad. I was sitting on the old orange step-stool in the garage one day, trying to explain to Mister .38 that getting out of Texas was just about the best thing that ever happened to me when I saw the neighbor's bloody shovel lying under his box hedge. The puppy was there, too. Both parts. Who would do such a thing, I asked Mister .38.

Nothing's worth anything unless you can get away from it. The problem is money. Having it. Getting it. Keeping it. Losing it. Loving it. Leaving it. Money. Some even run from it, from money itself, which, no surprise, requires money. But you can get away from that, too, if you know people in West Des Moines, Iowa.

By the time you get out of Texas and into West Des Moines, everything's taken care of, problems sorted, checks posted, accounts dissolved. Shit, by the time you show up in West Des Moines, you don't even exist anymore. And, when you wake up on a beat-to-hell futon in your friend Max Latham's basement, you feel like you can say just what this world is worth—because there it is, way behind you. There's nothing left but dust, the futon, some bookshelves, and the sound of water running in the kitchen above. Everything you know, you've gotten away from, and that, my friend, is living.

Unfortunately, if you then make the mistake of getting married, it's all downhill from there. At the bottom of the hill is a house in California one block away from a polluted beach, a wife who hates you, a lot of remorse, and a decapitated puppy. But you're not there yet. You're still, at present, stuck deep in the bad reality of getting out of Texas the hard way, which means getting out for good and for good reason—with bullets somehow involved and, for all you know, with that good reason back up the highway behind you, coming on strong. Right now, you're into more than just a speeding U-Haul, because Jackson Jackson is driving and that special goodness behind you might just be the Texas Rangers. Not the ball team.

Consider what you know about your old chum, Jackson Jackson: He's tall and thin. He does calisthenics every morning at five religiously no matter where he is and he always has for as long as you've known him. In the navy he was a forklift operator and a shotgun expert. He'd send you postcards from exotic locations where he'd had many drinks with beautiful local women. He's the only black man you've ever met who listens to *Rush*. In high school he ran track and laughed a lot, the kind of kid who'd give you the last dollar in his pocket and not mention it. But now, Jackson Jackson has become a bitter motherfucker. Now he keeps a .38 somewhere on him at all times, which he addresses as "Mister .38." He has a .44 in the luggage and a disassembled AK-47, which he calls *Kalashnikov* as if it were the lost testament of Jesus and Jackson Jackson just got religion.

"Treat *Kalashnikov* with respect," he'd say, then wink with a smile that was more like shorthand for some wrong, homicidal mission-statement he'd learned in the navy: *I'm gonna operate my forklift, clean my shotgun, then do you like you've never been done before.* Or, at least, that's how it seemed when he'd mention the AK. "Finest quality," he'd say. "Superior workmanship."

Consider that he'd been out of the navy for six days; that you hadn't seen him in person for six years; that his grandmother, who'd raised him, had just died; and that there were large bullet holes all over the back of the U-Haul. Say to yourself: there is no causal connection between these things. Granted, his grandmother died of natural causes. She was very old. One does not, however, acquire bullet holes through natural causes. When asked, Jackson Jackson's only response was to nod and say, "I know. Shit's fucked-up."

Indeed.

Now say you're me. That's the situation in which I found myself: shit = all fucked up. I contemplated the variables from the passenger's seat as dead-flat Texas got rainsoaked to the horizon, and my old friend stared straight ahead, pissed at past, present, and future all at once.

Consider the piano that fell out the back of the truck and hit the highway. It was interesting. The whole thing exploded, wood going everywhere, keys, the big metal harp inside clanging down over its hammers in the middle lane. It was fun to watch it all burst apart in the side mirror. In the rain, the fragments sticking up at odd angles reminded me of a shipwreck. Jackson Jackson looked in his mirror, held his hand out for the whiskey bottle, and said nothing.

We were both sweating. Outside, it was fifty degrees and pouring but, in the truck, it was Cabo San Lucas at peak tourist season. The heat hadn't worked for the first thirty minutes out of Austin. Trying to get it going, I'd turned it up all the way and broke the switch. Now, if we rolled the windows down, we got a big Texas facial. So there we were: drinking Black Velvet and losing weight by the mile.

"Well," I said, "we're almost to Dallas."

"Bed's about to go."

He was right. It took me a second before I saw the top sheet fluttering around the side like a white flame. His grandma's big, oak four-poster bed with the carved lion feet. She'd just had too much stuff. We'd tied the door down with a bungee cord, but that didn't even hold it to Buford Station, and the door's bent latch kept coming open.

"You want to stop again?" I asked, reaching to turn down the *Beach Boys Reunion*, the only tape besides *Doctor Hook and the Medicine Show* we could get at the BI-LO in Martenville. It got stuck in the tape player and auto-reversed at the end of each side in spite of all my attempts to pry it out.

"Do *not* touch that fucking dial."

"We better stop," I said.

He handed me the bottle without looking and put the truck in fourth. The lead Beach Boy, the one who got fat and started looking like a latterday Spanky, sang *she's giving me excitations*. It was the seventeenth time we'd listened to the song, but Jackson Jackson wouldn't let me turn it off, wallowing in his misery.

I guess he missed his grandmother. I'd talked to her a few times back when Jackson Jackson and I were in high school in LA. She seemed like a nice lady, but I couldn't imagine why she'd moved to Austin. Jackson Jackson didn't know anybody in Texas. She raised him, but he didn't say anything about her funeral or his family when he asked me to go along. He just said, "She's got this glass bar, right? And it's real nice. We could set it up in the basement."

Possibly, I came along just to help him out. Possibly, it was also convenient that I was leaving Texas, too. But the world wouldn't weep for one less upright piano, and I was pretty sure we'd have to sell that bed off or put it on the roof because it wasn't going to fit through the front door of Max Latham's house.

Max was waiting in Iowa with open arms and open basement. Everybody needs an old high school friend with a wife, a stable job, and an empty basement. It's necessary when the navy's made you weird. Or, in my case, when you went off to study writing and philosophy, but wound up in Texas with a large gambling debt and no gainful employment.

When the bed hit the highway, it didn't shatter like the piano. It went down *crunch-crunch* on all four lion feet, and there it was, linens flapping in the rain around the triple band of silver electrical tape we'd put down to keep everything in place.

"They don't make them like that anymore," I said. "Crashworthy."

Jackson Jackson pulled a three-point turn suddenly and with such vehemence it almost tipped us over.

"You had to say that," he said.

It took us an hour and a half to put the bed back in and tie it down.

Close my eyes. She's so much closer now. Softly smile, I know she must be kind.

I woke up on the couch as usual, went into the kitchen, and made a cup of instant coffee. I couldn't stop thinking about the puppy. I'd dreamt its severed head was licking my hand.

The bedroom door was locked, of course, and that was a good thing. Maybe Gary was in there right now sleeping blissfully in the arms of my wife. My wife: Max Latham's former wife. A year ago, I'd been in the Gary Position. Now I was in the Max Position. Did it serve me right? Had anything ever served Jackson Jackson right on our fateful trip, his short trajectory from navy to Iowa basement to bullets to Ft. Madison State Penitentiary?

Maybe it was time for Mister .38 to finally have a coming-out party. Maybe three shots for Cheryl and three for Gary, Jackson Jackson style. Then a quick reload and six more in the ceiling as I howled and did a crazed, murderous hat dance. El Danceo de Vengeance. But the door was locked and closed. Whatever was behind it was still awash in a haze of quantum possibilities: Gary? Cheryl? Some other guy? Another headless house pet? The string section of the Chicago Symphony Orchestra all pressed together cheek by jowl, their instruments held gingerly above their heads as if they were fording a river? Maybe. But I didn't have to deal with it if I didn't see it. So I decided to take my coffee down a block and talk to the ocean.

Imperial Beach stunk. Literally. The sand itself smelled like a fouled toilet, and there were red signs saying TOXIC and HAZARD at the end of every street going to the cement boardwalk. The beach had been critically polluted going on four months, blocked-up toilets in Mexico, overflowing sewers, sending the shit north. But toxic sand never killed anybody through their feet. And brown tide hadn't killed the surfers. You could see it in the waves. The whitewater wasn't white. Yet the kids were out on their boards, surfin' the break every day.

I curled my toes into the sand, sipped my coffee, stared at gray morning. "What do you expect me to do?" I asked the beach. "What's required when a man catches his wife blatantly cheating it up?" I looked to the brown tide for answers. Asking the tide was crazy. It didn't make sense. But what made sense? Forty-five minutes south of San Diego, Imperial Beach was the broke-ass redheaded stepchild of Southern California. Gang members didn't even come there anymore due to the stench. But the locals kept walking their dogs every morning in pathetic imitation of the beautiful crowd up north. The surfers still surfed.

I heard, "Dude!" as two overtanned kids came out of the water holding their boards. These were the same kids with the same boards saying the same *Dude!* that you'd find on any beach, except here the kid on the left was picking toilet paper out of his waistband instead of kelp. "Nasty," said the other. I smiled and nodded as they passed. Nasty was right. And, more importantly, somebody close by had whacked that puppy. I wondered who. That was something Jackson Jackson, at his lowest, might have done.

It's a fifteen-hour drive from Austin to West Des Moines. After six hours, I took the wheel but decided to stop when I realized I was driving on the wrong side of the highway. Jackson Jackson just laughed, turned up *Surf Safari*, and said, "No, man, just keep on going. We'll get there." But we were on one of those long stretches of dark Texas nothing, where you can see a light from a great distance. And not seeing one, not seeing anything through the rain-glittered windshield but fifty feet of highway caught in the headlights, made me nervous.

"I don't feel right," I said, pulling over to the side.

"Doesn't stop *me* day-to-day."

"Too many variables. I'm too tired. Let's get some sleep."

He didn't say anything to that. I closed my eyes and tried to get comfortable in the seat. Time passed in blessed post-Beach Boys silence. The air seemed cleansed now that the tap of rain on the truck had replaced *a bushy bushy blond hairdo*. I also had the slosh of the Black Velvet bottle to remind me that Jackson Jackson did not share my views on sleep as opposed to facing the dark infinity of Texas. I hoped he'd drink the rest of the BV and pass into whiskey dreamland. Jackson Jackson hungover couldn't have been that different from Jackson Jackson sober. And I wondered if it was all just the Navy and his grandmother. I wondered what had happened in the last six years to change him so drastically and so much for the worse.

Of course, he did sleep eventually. When I woke up sometime in the late morning, he was out with the empty bottle upright on the floor between his feet. I had the overall lousy feeling of having slept in the driver's seat of a U-Haul. But, all things considered, there was no harm done and soon we would be out of Texas, which brought a certain joy to my heart.

I was so confident, in fact, that I thought it would be a good time to call Maddog, the man to whom I owed a total of $17,870 as a result of the three worst poker games of my life. I didn't own a cell phone for many good reasons, so I took Jackson Jackson's out of the ashtray and dialed Maddog from memory.

How I got involved with a man named Maddog is, in itself, a tale to be told. Suffice it to say, there are still a few ways left to struggle without having to get a soul-destroying, ass-numbing nine-to-five. And one of those ways, apart from murder or dealing mountains of drugs out the trunk of your car, is card playing. You just have to have patience and sit in the small games until you meet the right people who can hook you up with the bigger games. You also have to be good, and you have to have enough honesty with yourself to know whether you are. That's where Maddog came in. He didn't play cards; he played money. I told myself I was good enough to borrow his, pay my debts, make my rent, and pay his back. I told myself that three times in a row and, all three times, I was lying.

"I don't know you," was how he answered the phone. Okay: Caller ID, cell phone technology and all that meant he could see who was calling, and he didn't know Jackson Jackson from Adam (good for Jackson Jackson). But the real reason Maddog answered that way was that he didn't associate with one single respectable person. He was something out of a B-gangster film, and he did the things that B-gangsters in films did. Maddog wasn't from Austin. He was from Queens. He sounded every bit of it when he answered.

"Maddog. It's Christian."

"You fucking rat bastard."

"Yeah, about that—"

"Now is not time for the bullshit, Christian. Bring my money over right now, and you'll be glad you did."

"I'm on vacation. I won't be around for a while. I hope that doesn't put you out."

"I'll find you. Don't worry about that."

"God bless you, Maddog. You're a Mother Teresa. You know that? A big, goddamn, stupid, stinking Mother Teresa who doesn't know when to quit. Pretty soon, you'll be nailing the sick in Calcutta."

"I get my hands on you, and it won't be so funny."

Why did I take the trouble to agitate the idiotic, leg-breaking asshole who was right then scouring the Austin card rooms for the faintest scent of my trail? I don't know. Maybe, in my own way, I was equally as stupid. If he was a mad dog, I was a weasel. I'd just made the most weaselly phone call of my adult life. But it felt good. One last kiss-my-ass—coming from *me* this time—as I vanished into the comforting embrace of God's own American Midwest.

"There's a little more to you leaving Austin, huh?" Jackson Jackson still had his eyes closed, but his snoring had stopped.

"You want to tell me about the bullet holes in the back of the truck then? And we can have a heart-to-heart about all the heinous shit we're dealing with here?"

"Now I will piss." He climbed out on his side and pissed to the east. I climbed out on mine and pissed to the west. I had no doubt right then that, just like me, he was reviewing the unlikely and unfortunate events that had conspired to have both of us pissing on the same latitude.

Schopenhauer wrote: "The ordinary man places his life's happiness in things external to him, in property, rank, wife and children, friends, society, and the like, so that when he loses them or finds them disappointing, the foundation of his happiness is destroyed." I believe the Beach Boys put it this way: *I'm gettin' bugged driving up and down the same old strip/ I gotta find a new place where the kids are hip.* Just so. But putting my happiness elsewhere and moving on from Imperial Beach to the next thing, from Cheryl, who'd been Max Latham's unfaithful wife and who'd once seemed like my salvation, would not be easy or simple. She had a steady job as a RN at

Kaiser. I'd been *looking* for a job. The Accord was in her name. Since I rolled it, I only used it when she didn't need it. She put all the money we'd stolen from Max toward a down payment on the house. If I walked, where would I go? I'd be sleeping in the Greyhound Bus Terminal. External things? Yes. When I got back home from the ocean, Cheryl was having it out with Gary in the living room.

Gary was in boxers and a T-shirt. Strangely, he was also wearing brown loafers with brown dress socks. My wife was in panties and a *Cal* sweatshirt I'd never seen before. Her long brown hair was only partly tied back, and she had the same fierce, wide-eyed expression as the day she'd done half a bag of speed and threatened the mailman.

"I saw you," she said. "You think I don't know where you go?"

Gary crossed his arms. "A lot of people look like me from a distance. Right, Christian?"

I glanced from Gary to Cheryl. The fact that he was fucking her was one thing. I was ready for that. But backing him up in an argument? I wasn't ready. I thought about running for the safety of the garage and my little orange step-stool.

"Don't bring him into this." She crossed her own arms, squared her stance, shaking a little from the dope she'd obviously done. "He can't even get it up."

What?

"I think you're paranoid. I think you've got a substance habit," he said.

"Asshole," she screamed as she ran back into the bedroom. "I'm gonna find that bitch and cut her bitch heart out."

"You do that, but don't call me when you're down for assault. Find somebody who cares."

I sat on the couch and looked at the brown hairline cracks on the bottom of my coffee cup. I felt like a kid again, watching my parents.

"Screw you." Cheryl had put on some jeans. She stormed through the living room and out the front door. The screen slammed behind her with a *thwack*.

We listened to the car peel out.

Now the house was silent. Gary sat down on the other end of the couch and stared at the gray TV screen.

"Women," he said.

I went into the kitchen and put my cup in the sink. It was a mess. Nothing had been cleaned in weeks. There was the smell of death from the overstuffed garbage disposal. We didn't have any utensils in the utensil drawer. I wondered where they'd gone and had the crazy thought that maybe my wife had gotten guilty and sent all the cutlery back to Max. All I saw was a wine corkscrew with a burgundy-stained cork on it and a couple of small, water-spotted paring knives.

Gary turned on some basketball and settled in with his hand in his boxers. I walked over and sat down on the arm of the couch. "This is for the puppy," I said and stabbed him in the stomach.

"Fuck," he said. "What the fuck did you do that for?"

The paring knife had gone in about a quarter of an inch. It was the first time I'd ever stabbed someone. It wasn't as easy as I thought.

"I can get it up."

Gary looked at me and nodded, pressing his hand over the wound. "I believe you."

I gave him a hard stare before I went to the bathroom for the hydrogen peroxide and some Band-Aids.

We were over halfway there. Hours of fields and flat, open nothing: Toline, Eagle, Lungerberg, Gainesville. Dallas sliding past in the gray flash of morning. Rain coming down, then not, then again, ice-cold, fat Texas drops as big as the locusts that could storm up in summer and band the flesh off a grown cow.

Jackson Jackson had found a pair of black leather gloves somewhere in the luggage. They creaked as he tightened his jaw and tightened his grip on the wheel.

"I put those holes in the back of the truck before you showed up, okay?"

He said it spontaneously somewhere outside of Baton Springs. I pictured him with those gloves on, screaming incoherent syllables in his grandmother's front yard, firing round after round from *Kalashnikov* into the back of the U-Haul.

I asked him why. He thought of what he wanted to say. And I waited, watching the scrub go from Texas brown to Oklahoma red. The Beach Boys sang with gravity and passion about a little deuce coupe, and Maddog rang Jackson Jackson's phone for what must have been the twentieth time. We were a happy caravan of goodness. Even then, I pitied Max Latham for the sorrow that was clearly about to descend on his head.

"I broke my old fishbowl."

I nodded, but it made no sense. Fishbowl?

Just as all men need a former high school friend who's married and stable, so the friend needs to know better. Usually, the wife says something like, *oh no, they're not moving into* my *basement*—if she's a good woman, if she's done her wifely duty in distancing her man from all his old hoodlum friends. But I would find that Cheryl was not a good woman, and the shot-up U-Haul was raging down the interstate like Satan's private livery. What would happen, I wondered, when Max's wife saw the beaten, claw-footed bed with all its linens duct-taped in place? How would we account for the bullet hole-fish bowl connection? For the leather gloves? For the whiskey-sweat reek of the cab still pulsing with heat and Beach Boys perdition? No, it wouldn't do. We were all wrong.

Oklahoma passed with crops and sprinklers, with the smell of pesticide and fertilized soil. Then we were on the I-35 North, crossing into Kansas. At about that time, I concluded that everything about the fishbowl story was complete and utter bullshit. Maybe it was Kansas clearing out the last of Texas, the last part that had slipped up into Oklahoma as the South tried to rise. Kansas was rational. Kansas knew: one does not put a clip of 7.62 mm into the air over a fishbowl. Not even an emotional Naval forklift operator and shotgun expert would do such a thing. Maybe I'd lost my judgment for a while in the unreality of the trip, but my mind started coming back when Jackson Jackson answered one of Maddog's calls.

"Yes, hello, can I help you?" His all-professional-and-polite-noon-in-the-haberdashery-voice.

I stared at Jackson Jackson, but he just winked and gave me a minty smile. I could hear Maddog screaming on the other end, but I couldn't make out the words.

"503 Pearl Street, West Des Moines, Iowa." I heard a black leather glove creak on the wheel. "You got it, buddy." And Jackson Jackson hung up. He seemed deeply pleased with himself, smiling at the distance as if all the joy in the world had now become his.

I said: "You realize Maddog wants to kill me. You did realize that before you gave him our destination."

Jackson Jackson kept smiling. "Don't worry," he said. "I got guns."

I was behind the wheel because Gary felt too fragile to drive.

"Shouldn't we be armed for this sort of thing?"

"We're just looking," I said. "You know, for a lawyer, you're a nervous bastard. What are you trying to be, some kind of gangster?"

He winced and looked to see if there was blood on the palm of his hand. "I got stabbed today," he said.

I'd done a good job with the Band-Aids, but Gary still kept his hand pressed on his stomach as if his guts might shoot out at any minute. We were sitting in his forest green Jeep Cherokee across the street from Cheryl's favorite bar, The Brig. She'd been in there over an hour.

"Quit complaining. I should have killed you."

"Over her?"

We looked at each other.

"Did you behead that puppy in my backyard?"

Gary checked his palm again. "That's disgusting," he said. "Don't talk like that. It's bad luck to even hear something like that."

I looked him over and shook my head. "Somebody did. Puppies don't behead themselves."

"Maybe *she* did it."

Cheryl stumbled out through the tinsel in the bar's doorway. Behind her came a large man in jeans and a flannel shirt. He was grinning like he'd just won the state lottery and had nothing to do with the money but refurbish his trailer. We sat in silence as my wife leaned back against her Honda and made out with today's lucky number. Watching her, I knew deep in the cockles of my own small, criminal heart that the last bit of attraction I carried for this woman had just lifted away, replaced by a certain cold revulsion. I thought of our neighbor, Willis, knocked through a tree and her saying it was too bad. I thought of the puppy. Of Jackson Jackson's grandmother silent in her grave under Texas rain.

I moaned, and Gary shot me a startled look. I moaned the way I imagine Jackson Jackson might have moaned when he gunned down Maddog in the street in front of Max Latham's house. Moaned, not for Cheryl or a broken fishbowl or the polluted tide that never had any answers, but for all the choices I'd made that had put me on this latitude and for the cruel gravity that conspired to hold me to it.

"Don't do anything crazy," said Gary. "I'm an officer of the court." He winced and checked his palm. "I live by morality."

My wife and Lucky had gotten in her car and were pulling away. I started up the engine. "No," I said, "you live by me. And you fuck my wife." I hit the gas and the Cherokee surged. A red Honda Accord is no match for a green Jeep Cherokee in a collision. We sheared off her trunk and the Accord skidded up onto the sidewalk, bent trunk hood bouncing over nothing. I hoped Lucky would jump out so I could run him over, but Cheryl was still going on a snootful of speed that no amount of Brig drinks could negate. Smoke came off her back tires. She shot down the street, new friend and bouncing hood notwithstanding. In about three seconds, I was right behind her. Gary had stopped pressing his stomach and was now holding onto the dashboard and handbrake for the grace of god and deliverance from evil.

"The trouble is," I said as I put the pedal all the way down and rammed the back of the Honda, "the puppy was innocent. It didn't do anything to anybody. It just wanted to be loved." I hit my wife's car again and it fishtailed, rims flying, the back left tire wobbling badly.

Gary's mouth moved, but no sounds came out. It was all too much for him. I might have looked at him too long, too long as in one millisecond over. The road veered sharply to the right, I looked away from Gary and saw the edge coming, tried to turn, heard him pull up on the handbrake. There was a soft, empty moment where the Jeep Cherokee became a feather floating in a white nothing. All the fluids in my body began to rise, as we went over the edge of a canyon.

I wanted to speak. There was no time to speak. The front of the Jeep became my nose, the windshield my eyes, the steering wheel my cheeks, my mind the sky, my anger a dark, fiery cloud rolling upwards without sound. The rain of blood inside the Jeep made me think back to Texas one last time—one last, nervous thought that yanked me sideways into black.

Max Latham's house in the blue light of morning. And Max standing there watering his lawn as if the storm wasn't moving north from Texas. Anyone who thought to look could have seen it rolling up on the edge of the horizon like a polluted tide, bringing with it all manner of flotsam, heavily armed fools in U-Hauls, homicidal moneylenders from Queens, and 100,000 mgs of unmerciful fate delivered right to his front door. But that was exactly Max's problem. He never thought to look.

When we got out and walked up behind him, he was talking to Cheryl. She was sitting on the sill of the second-story bedroom window in jeans and a bra, smoking. Max absently held the hose to the side. The water bored a hole in the grass and puddled around his sneakers.

"Well, don't close the windows, then. I don't want my ass blown off in the middle of the night."

"Radon doesn't do that," said Cheryl. "It kills you in your sleep. You'd never know." She exhaled a tongue of smoke that hung over the porch for a moment before twisting into a draft.

Jackson Jackson and I stood behind Max and said nothing. Cheryl gave us an empty look and took another drag.

"Oh, that's so much better. I'm so happy. Die in my sleep. Fuck." Max gestured with the hose and pebble-sized clumps of water flew in an arc.

Then he turned and saw us. His expression changed from the morose Midwestern husband with receding, close clipped, blond hair and wire-rimmed glasses, to a boy delighted that his sandcastle had withstood the waves after all—complete with toothy grin and mud on his shoes. His old friends had arrived. No amount of radon could change that.

Max: the image of a chump, a fall guy, a perpetual victim. In school he'd been the one who got tricked, a bewildered, hurt expression on his face, as the bus pulled away. Yet there was always a streak of cheerfulness in him that enabled him to forgive everyone, to make it all right again. Seeing him made me want to smile, to clap him on the shoulder and celebrate something—maybe his innate goodness, maybe just the contrast between him and me. I may have fallen in love with his wife a little later. But, then again, I may have fallen in love with her at first sight, seeing her sitting up in the window, smoking, like she didn't care about a thing. Max was oblivious from the start. He had a paunch and obsessed about things like invisible gas poisoning, EMFs, and keeping a perfectly well-groomed front lawn. Many times during that first night, as we unpacked the truck and got extremely drunk, he grinned at the lawn and said, "Isn't that a fucking gorgeous piece of grass right there?"

Toward the end of the night, I think he may have hugged his front yard, but he could have simply fallen facedown on it, spread-eagled as if the whiskey and PBR had temporarily reversed all local gravity and the lawn was the only thing that cared enough to keep him from floating away. Max had been married for four or five months. I wondered how long he'd had his lawn.

We piled everything in the basement, everything, that is, except the bed, which we had to leave in the driveway under a tarp. Jackson Jackson said little. When I asked him how he felt about leaving the bed out, his only response was: "Light the fucker on fire." His mood, apparently, had not improved by arriving in West Des Moines.

No one lit the fucker on fire, but staggering drunk down the long, railless basement stairs at 3:00 in the morning with a tiny flashlight, I saw our mountains of boxes piled like miniature ziggurats in the dark, a tiny Babylon. Toward the center of the darkness, Jackson Jackson was snoring on the futon, probably with arms crossed like King Tut and a loaded gun in each hand. I passed out in the corner. I hoped, away from existing lines of fire.

Sometime in the wee hours of the morning, Max and Cheryl had a horrendous argument. I woke with the spins, my stomach lurching, and remembered hearing them screaming at each other and slamming things around. I would eventually discover that she threw his computer through one of the upper windows that morning and Max spent the rest of the dark hours cruising around town in his brown El Camino as he listened to Dwight Yoakum and drank more beer. The way she told it to me later was that she'd kicked him out of the house and it hadn't been the first time.

Problems. The first was extricating myself from the airbag. I came to upside down, the mouse-gray pillow almost suffocating me. The second problem was Gary. He was out, belted in place. It looked like the passenger airbag had shot forcefully enough to break his nose or something else had. Gary's blood was everywhere. His forehead was dark red with it, and there was a little puddle of it just below his head on the Cherokee's roof liner. He moaned and snuffled, a bloody bubble popping in his nostril.

I squirmed out, went around and unbelted Gary and pulled him through the shattered passenger-side window. The Cherokee was on fire, a little fire. It had been the source of the black firecloud that I saw in the rearview mirror after we went end over end and landed on the canyon floor. As soon as I dragged Gary away, the gas tank exploded with a hollow thump into sparks and green-orange streaks of flame, jagged strips of glass, and sizzling plastic.

Neither of us had cell phones. So I turned Gary on his side, leaned back into the ice plant and sticker weed on the slope of the canyon, and watched the Cherokee cook. A burning vehicle in the middle of a residential area: someone would call. There would be firetrucks, police, ambulance. Gray wheezed and snorted blood. I watched a sea gull glide over the rooftops of houses on the other side of the canyon.

Two hours passed, and Gary grew silent. I couldn't tell if he was alive or dead. I put my ear to his back and still couldn't tell. No one arrived. No sirens in the distance. Nothing but the occasional gull overhead, the smell of melted plastic.

So I did the only other thing I could do. I walked. People don't like people who walk away. It's unpopular. It's ugly. It shows a certain changeability, weakness, lack of determination. I didn't feel good about it, but I went anyway. I left (blood-spattered, probably dead) Gary on the slope of the canyon and walked my way to freedom. Or, if not to freedom, then at least out of a certain kind of bondage that would have involved explaining to police how we'd arrived at the bottom of the canyon in the first place. I told myself repeatedly it was actually good that no one called or came, that Gary got what he deserved.

The ice plant roots were twisted like rigging, and even though I was beaten and dizzy, they enabled me to climb right up and out of the canyon. I went down the sidewalk, wondering what I was going to do now that I had no home.

Late afternoon and nobody was on the street. It was a quiet residential neighborhood not far from the beach. Little brightly colored one-story houses. Kids' toys strewn on front lawns. Three-foot high white picket fences. Party sounds came from a backyard, pool splashes, laughter. Pure bright clouds hung low in the hard blue sky. I went down the driveway of a house towards the party sounds, half-thinking that I should say something to someone about Gary, half-thinking that it would be nice to lie down next to a pool where people are laughing and sleep. I had a powerful urge to sleep.

Three metallically clean, blond teenagers tossed a beach ball in the pool, two girls and a boy. They looked happy and perfect like models, like they'd been pressed from a mold. On the far side of the pool, another boy was grilling burgers. A tiny CD player with speakers plugged into it played music I'd never heard before, a crackly kind of accelerated country with the singer whispering nervously over the guitar.

I sat down in a white chaise longue and looked at them. Eventually, the boy and girls in the pool waded towards me. They didn't get out. The boy on the other side looked over but kept grilling. The music scraped out of the speakers on the patio table next to me as the singer stammered and strummed his guitar. I caught lyrics about love and radiation coming from the sky.

"You're bloody," said one of the girls.

I turned my head slightly to see her, realizing that there was something wrong with my neck.

"Who messed you up?" asked the boy in the pool next to her.

I noticed that there was a tear across the filthy bloodstained button-down that had been white when I'd bought it long ago at the Austin JC Penney. The boy who'd been grilling came around and stood next to the CD player, holding the grilling fork with a smoking hamburger patty stuck on the prongs. I looked up and smiled. The boy in the pool took a step back.

Maddog was on his way. Jackson Jackson had already cleaned and assembled the AK in anticipation and was sitting down in the basement, testing the firing action and loading clips with black-jacketed 7.62 mm cartridges that looked more like a bad day in Baghdad than home defense. Jackson Jackson looked like a bad day in Baghdad. He'd never been more cheerful, but with that crisp smile that was heavier on the homicide than the happy. I knew he wouldn't be after Max's wife. Everything that had formerly been Jackson Jackson the human had gotten jettisoned into some distant, pockmarked landscape in a USMC Government Issue Standard Waste Disposal Receptacle. All that was left was Jackson Jackson the Pile of Endless Rage with the occasional episode of Malicious Joy thrown in by the gods for flavor.

I don't know what it is about upheaval that makes people seek it out, or what it is about very personal, very utter destruction that makes people hungry for it like no other. But I knew then, in the way of knowing that seems completely clear, even though it's completely corrupt, just how good Cheryl looked to me when I staggered up from the basement the next morning, my hair like a bush hit by too much wind.

Was I corrupt or just aware? Why was it that neither Jackson Jackson nor Max had any desire for this well-endowed brunette, who, as I emerged from the basement, happened to be drinking a beer in her underwear—very narrow, very sexy black underwear? She leaned back against the kitchen sink and gave me a look so clear and blank her eyes might have been polished glass—the same look she'd given me from the window the day before. As we stood there blinking at each other, I wondered what it would be like waking up next to her legs, what her belly would look like when she stretched and arched her back.

Right then, I should have jumped in the U-Haul, turned up the Beach Boys, and wailed through the cornfields until inertia and gas mileage won and all there was was an atomized pin-flat duskline as far as I could look, the nearest telephone pole fifty miles gone. Then I should have started to run. I knew this just like I knew the house was ready to pop with Max hungover upstairs facedown in his bed and Jackson Jackson in the basement getting ready for war. He'd traded up the Beach Boys for *Funk Soul Brother* on infinite repeat as he kissed each cartridge and whispered to it before grinning and sliding it into the clip.

Yes. Crazy. But all I could think was how cool Cheryl was, drinking a beer all by herself in the kitchen at noon in her black underwear and not giving a shit.

"No," she said, "you don't get a beer. This is the last one."

"I wasn't asking."

She raised an eyebrow and put the empty bottle in the sink. "This, from someone living rent-free in my basement?"

"Don't worry about the money. It'll flow like sweet milk from heaven as soon as we stock the bar down there and get our liquor license."

"Funny man."

Nobody who says *funny man* ever means it the way it sounds. It's always a placeholder for something else, some other stronger observation that can't be voiced right then. What I didn't realize, as Cheryl moved close to me and rested her palm lightly on my chest, was that she was about to kiss me.

When I become a learned philosopher, my first book will be entitled *The Beach Boys as Ontological Modality: An American Response to Schopenhauer's Primacy of Will*. I will argue that the term "hodaddies," as it occurs, for example, in the song "Surfers Rule," is a mystery term, an intentionally ambiguous sign, carrying a multiplicity of culturally significant meanings: *The hodaddies sittin' while the surfers are draggin'/The surfers are winnin' and they say as they're grinnin'/Surfers rule*. Hodaddies. What does Schopenhauer have to say in response to hodaddies? That angle has been completely overlooked by scholars. It will be the first of many important books I will write. The second will be an exploration of death. Specifically, how little deaths create chain reactions that result in big deaths. I will reference hodaddies.

Hodaddy No. 1: Little fluffy puppy that didn't have a name. The puppy that haunted my dreams, severed head, blood crusted into white fur.

Hodaddy No. 2: Max Latham, who now also haunts me in his own sad way, who stumbled downstairs too late to catch his wife kissing me, who, like the puppy, only ever wanted to be loved and free to focus on harmful minerals in the tap water and the hygiene of his front lawn. He didn't ask for nihilistic, ex-naval shotgun experts and failed gamblers. Max didn't ask for philandering wives in sexy black underwear. But this world is full of victims. And so there would come a time when the puppy would have to lose its head, Max his wife, Jackson Jackson his freedom, Maddog his life, and me my immortal soul.

And then, of course, Hodaddio Grande del Mundo: the flight of bullets through the air, cyclic rate of fire as estimated by the US Department of Defense: 650-750 rounds per minute, give or take variations in barrel design that might affect velocity. The grand Hodaddy doing its thing over your rental car, the street, up the front of your body, and out the back.

"Where's Jackson?" Max asked, not even noticing that Cheryl was standing there in her black underwear or maybe not even caring since their fight the night before.

She shrugged, and the glimmer of interest I'd seen in her face when she kissed me receded into the mask of blank indifference that seemed to be her normal state—and would be until much later, when she'd discover she liked to do speed with various unwashed individuals in the washroom of The Brig.

"I think he's downstairs, loading his weapons," I said.

"Oh." Max frowned deeply and poured distilled water into the coffeepot by the sink, blinking his bloodshot eyes slowly against the light. I wondered how much was hangover and how much was anxiety that the trouble with his wife or maybe the brooding arsenal in the basement would somehow negatively impact his lawn. How could a man who was ingenious enough to build a tri-level water distiller in his kitchen from hardware store parts and a battery pack completely overlook his wife? Or, for that matter, how could he overlook the very depressed, dangerous man sitting in his basement giving each bullet its own unique name?

Max put the grounds in, turned it on, and the smell of percolating coffee filled the air. For that moment, as the three of us stood there blinking at each other, I hoped it all might work out. I told myself I'd legitimately put Texas behind me. I could get a straight job, pay off my debts, maybe get a lawn of my own. Max had to know something the rest of us didn't. Unfortunately, the moment after that, I realized Jackson Jackson was not still in the basement loving his bullets. He was in the street outside, firing them.

We ran out like idiots. I saw Maddog on his back in the street, red long-sleeved button-down shirt, sneakers pointing up, and jeans washed in blood. His scraggly beard. His fat belly. A pistol in his left hand. His eyes staring straight up at Holy Astral Queens, the loan shark heaven. I didn't feel good about him dying, but then I didn't feel bad about me living. And it looked like Jackson Jackson wasn't feeling anything, standing there like a statue with *Kalashnikov* smoking.

The bullet holes were large. The same ones that covered

the back of the U-Haul had riddled Maddog's rented Taurus. Jackson Jackson frowned at them as if they'd failed to live up to his expectations point by point. He was a death artist, and this was his performance, his installation in the center of 503 Pearl Street, with cordite in the air and Max back inside, sweating and pissing and hissing an emergency-911-death-immediately-now hodaddy into the telephone.

Jackson Jackson sat down right where he was, in a half-lotus, and proceeded to disassemble and clean each part of his weapon with a little white bristle brush and a can of machine oil from his pocket. When the SWAT team arrived, no shots were fired. A gun-cleaning kit was confiscated along with the AK parts and several pockets of ammo.

The next day, Max didn't go to work and started drinking at 8 AM. No one had been shot in front of his house before, and he was taking it hard. He sat in the den, sipping whiskey as he clicked the TV remote with a trembling hand. The fact that he'd started on a brand-new bottle of Black Velvet was not lost on me. So many synchronicities seemed present when I realized he was watching a biography on Dennis Wilson, the Beach Boys' drummer. Everything comes together. Everything converges. I said it to myself over and over. This is not a chaotic, disconnected whirlwind of shit and suffering. There are reasons. There is a tide, even if it happens to be brown. If you don't want to ask the tide, ask Schopenhauer. He'll tell it true.

I kept saying this all to myself when I crept down into the basement to do some secret packing and found Cheryl waiting there with one suitcase full of money and another full of clothes. My clothes. My suitcases. Max's money. It looked like *all* of Max's money. She unzipped my little blue valise and showed me how she'd rolled the twenties and fifties in fat little bundles, each one like something a movie gangster would have in his pocket after selling a pound of crack. How many pounds would this represent? It looked like harvest day in Crackland.

"I love beautiful women smiling at me with suitcases full of cash," I said, "but I hate jail and, oh, who knows, bounty hunters and enraged husbands and death."

Cheryl shrugged. "I don't give a fuck, and I won't offer twice. Max is an asshole. He deserves it."

Maybe seeing Jackson Jackson take out Maddog in the street jarred something loose. Maybe she was just as fundamentally evil and crazy as everyone else, sexiness notwithstanding. But such a woman in such a situation making such an offer could seem right even if it were wrong. No matter the reasons, in a life of lousy decisions, leaving with her seemed like the answer, the next thing. Everything comes together.

"When?"

"Tonight."

"How?"

"I've got a car." Cheryl zipped the suitcase back up. "This is everything. I've been planning this. Max is screwed right now, but he doesn't even realize it. He won't have time to come looking."

I nodded. She smiled. And then we, too, came together. A few hours later, we were gone.

These things. Convergences, mistakes and imperfections, resurgences, corrections, convections, exceptions. The slow path of a leaf or a bullet through the air. And I ask myself who the puppy is: Gary, Jackson Jackson, Max, or me. And who is West Des Moines? And who is the futon in the basement? Who are the bullets? And what is the problem? Money? And how are we getting away from it, Money? And gravity, why gravity, when all we want to do is leave?